The Paper Folders of Shitaké

Infernal Foxface

THE PAPER FOLDERS OF SHITAKÉ

COLE MACHIA

For Filly

The Paper Folders of Shitaké

Published by Infernal Foxface Books

Tombo no

Kusa ni undeya ⁻

Ushi no tsuno

O Dragonfly, how you have wearied of

The grass that you should thus perch

Upon the horn of a cow!

1

Mimura Tendō, learned samurai, gentle creature, and writer of the famous treatise on family relations of the nobles entitled "Footprints of the Four Winds", as well as many other classical works of poetry, tantric studies, meditations, and occasionally, brief biographical sketches. Founder of the famed school of the 'Unfettered Bridle', the most excellent sword stance which many a young samurai may thank for the keeping of their lives. Defender of the holy realm of Enchō, which, while under siege by the multitudinous, barbarous host of the Great Northern Way, seemed on the verge of total destruction--the peaceful inhabitants of

Enchō, their homes burnt, their fields salted, their women ravaged, and their sons crucified on the roadsides-saved, in most glorious fashion by this Mimura Tendō, who vanquished, personally and with his own blade, five hundred and thirty-two of the enemy of that holy realm until, finally, demoralized and their numbers fast dwindling, the armies of the Great Northern Way broke and fled, and have not been seen in this world since.

It was this Mimura Tendō; Tendō the fair, Tendō the honorable, who now screamed so loudly as the left side of his body separated itself from the right and plopped to the ground, spraying blood like that which would run at the scene of an epic battle, thanks to a single sword stroke by the most fair, and most honorable, Kimitaké Oin.

The noble blood of Mimura Tendō continued to spray into the air for some odd minutes until finally slowing to a low trickle which made the wheat underneath the two halves of the great man red as the morning sun. Kimitaké in did not look down at the body, focusing, instead, on the reflection of the sun at the tip of his sword. The blood of Mimura Tendō dripped down the length of the blade and congealed between his strong fingers as they firmly gripped the handle. A cicada, concealed by the field of wheat, began to cry. Kimitaké Oin slowly lowered his head and closed his eyes as he knelt by the body of Mimura Tendō, and then said, aloud, a prayer for the departing soul.

The wind blows…

through the leaves

The fireflies collect the lights

After saying this, Kimitaké stood up and ran his fingers through his straight long hair. The blood on his hands smeared into his hair, mixing with the dark brown color, and streaking it with a pinkish red. With his eyes squinted from the sun, his cheeks raised high, showing the hardness on the otherwise youthful face that most would call beautiful, he sighed as the wind blew through his kimono. The crest with a blue seagull fluttered into his vision as if it were a reminder of some ancient purpose. He caught the fluttering cloth and stared closely at the crest. Then upon releasing it, he wiped the blood from his blade with a clean white cloth, then let the wind take the cloth. He stood up straight and sheathed his sword and, puffing out his chest with a deep breath, he looked down at the body of Mimura Tendō.

"Once again, I am left without a rival," he said melancholically.

The blood slowly dripped from the mouth of the body, and the ribs, without the stability of a connecting sternum, fell limply, knocking together like a child's wind chime. Kimitaké Oin nodded, understanding this to be the soul of Mimura Tendō agreeing with his statement.

2

Lady Keiko sat rather inappropriately on her knees, gently folding a small square of colored paper into the fragile shape of a crane. She stuck her tongue partly out of her mouth and pinched it between her crimson lips, and her eyes narrowed until the carefully plucked eyebrows came together in an almost masculine fashion as she poured all her concentration into the paper folding, when the muffled sound of approaching footsteps forced Lady Keiko back into the world around her. Quickly, she grabbed the assorted scraps of paper lying in small stacks around her feet, representing already failed attempts to fold what in her mind would be the proper crane. She stuffed the paper noiselessly under a beaded cushion and placed her body over it as the footsteps came louder, and ended at her door. The silhouette of a young girl could be seen on the other side of the screen, and Lady Keiko gave out a loud sigh of relief.

"Ah, is that you Chikako? Please come in," she said in a friendly tone, but one that, nonetheless, spoke of her position of authority over the young girl. The door slid open with a smooth but static sound. The door seemed to slide open by itself due to the small, doll-like hands of Chikako. She was very easily hidden behind even the smallest of obstructions, which made her invaluable to Lady Keiko who, although not having taken the liberty yet, felt that at some time she might like the services of a spy; an almost invisible figure who could tell her all the secret goings on at the court, and whom Keiko felt to be a perfect candidate.

"Oh, Chikako, I am so happy it is you," she said in a light though monotonic voice; and, placing her hands on Chikako's knees, she stared into the girl's eyes. Lady Keiko always loved to stare into the eyes of Chikako. It always gave her the feeling one has on a rare holiday. The way the lights seemed to sparkle in the pupil, Lady Keiko had to fight the urge to turn and see if a hundred candles had not been secretly and instantly lit, and placed in a wide circle, surrounding the two as they sat facing one another. She then turned her head to the side and covered her slightly upturned nose with her fingers and, smiling, gave a girlish giggle.

"I am happy that my presence pleases you," said Chikako, her cheeks blushing, her voice highly pitched and fragile like that of a small child. "But may I ask, why is it you seemed so relieved?"

Lady Keiko giggled again, then took a deep breath and tried to hold it; but being unable to, she let the air out of her lungs and laughed. Her face flustered as she stared down at the pillow covering the sheets of paper she had hidden. She then pat her breast and said to the girl, "Chikako, do you have a fan with you? Please tell me you do."

"Of course," Chikako answered, and pulled a small paper fan from the white sash of her light blue kimono. The fan made a snapping noise as Chikako flipped it open with a slight movement of her wrist and began to fan a breeze over Lady Keiko whose forehead had begun to bead with sweat. Lady Keiko watched the fan as it rose into the air and came down again. There was a scene of the ocean painted onto it; waves breaking around shoreline rocks, and three seagulls flying overhead. As the fan moved, Lady Keiko could imagine the wings of the seagulls flapping, and the wind from the fan became that of the birds' wings.

"Is that Izu?" she asked, her voice barely a whisper.

"My Lady, I beg your pardon?" Chikako asked,

unable to comprehend the Lady Keiko's question.

"Oh, nothing," she answered, composing herself, and sitting upright. "But as to what you were asking, I suppose I was a bit pleased to see you now, wasn't I?" Chikako smiled and nodded her head. "Well then, I will tell you a secret," Lady Keiko continued. She looked suspiciously around at the paper paneling of the walls and leaned in close to the girl. "But you must promise not to tell a single soul. Do you promise?"

Chikako's bundled hair bobbed back and forth as she nodded her head quickly; too quickly for her to have thought about keeping any secrets. Lady Keiko hesitated, then slowly lifted the beaded pillow, revealing the hidden stash of papers. Chikako looked down curiously at the papers.

"I do not understand," said the girl.

Lady Keiko rubbed her hands over the papers, spreading them out on the matted floor, and giggled as she pushed the crumpled-up papers away from those unused. She picked up one of the clumsier folded cranes and, narrowing her eyes, she jokingly fluttered the paper bird in mock flight in front of Chikako's face. Chikako watched its movements as if they were spoken orders from her lady, which must be remembered word for word. Lady Keiko laughed once more, loudly.

"This is my secret," she said, and handed the

crane to the girl. Chikako stared confusedly it.

"Origami? But why are you keeping this secret?" she asked.

"Because my husband does not approve," answered Lady Keiko. "Lord Shitaké considers origami a bad habit if one does not do it well. He believes the struggle to perfect the art a representation of sexual frustration. It would embarrass him to have others see me in this way."

Chikako picked up several of the crumpled papers as Lady Keiko held up a scarlet-colored square, and held it in front of the candle, giving the room a strange red glow.

"I practice in secret so that he will not see my failed attempts," Lady Keiko continued.

"The crane is a hard piece to make," Chikako replied apologetically.

"You do not need to make excuses for me," Lady Keiko laughed. "I have no talent for it, it is that simple. But, if I continue to practice, I will improve."

"I am sorry," said Chikako, lowering her head, "but I still do not understand."

"Do not look so unhappy, dear Chikako. In fact, the origami is only part of my secret."

"Oh?"

"Yes. In fact, I am planning something, but I will need your help to make it work."

"I will do anything you ask," Chikako replied. Lady Keiko leaned in close once more.

"In three weeks, Lord Shitaké is going to announce a contest. An origami contest, to see who in all the province can fold the most beautiful designs." Chikako raised her head, a look of surprise on her face.

"He is?"

"Well, he will. Though he does not know it yet. This is why I need your help. I want to enter this contest. If I keep practicing in secret, by the time of the contest, I will be able to show that I have great skill. And since nobody will have seen me in my faltering attempts while practicing, everyone will assume that my talent is natural. And more importantly, the entire court will believe me to have no sexual frustration. Lord Shitaké will be pleased with this, I think."

"But how will he announce this contest not knowing he is going to do so?" Chikako asked. Lady Keiko reached out and stroked the girl on the cheek.

"My sweet Chikako. The Lord Shitaké is very easily persuaded. Certainly, he has no intention of announcing any contest; but if the idea were properly introduced to him, then his intentions could be easily changed."

Chikako closed her eyes and moved her head to the side as Lady Keiko continued to stroke her cheek, and asked in a low voice, "My Lady, how do you plan to persuade the Lord?"

Lady Keiko slowly lowered her hand from Chikako's soft cheek, and placed it gently on the girl's left breast, and said, "You are going to suggest it, while making love to him."

3

Hojo Ryu could remember plain as day the moment he met his beautiful wife, Noriko. Pale faced with pitch black hair and slightly bucked teeth; that's how he always imagined her with the bucked teeth, smiling. He loved her at first sight and, had even declined a dowry in order for them to wed. He declined a few other things as well; for, unfortunately, the couple were forced to elope. And even though that time had been extremely trying, and there had been moments when regret had crept in, Ryu could say, in all honesty, that that had been the happiest time of his life.

However, the memory of the night before last did not come plain as day, it came dark blue as the midnight sky on a new moon.

Once more, he looked down at the note Noriko

had left for him along with his rice balls and soup. In brief, the note began with a solemn declaration of her love for him, and then went on to explain how their only son, seven-year-old Kaoru, was, in fact, not his son at all but the son of another man, the Shogun Shitaké.

Ryu, in a fit of rage, crumpled up the note; then, with a gasp, he un-crumpled the paper and tried to flatten it out as much as he could, moving his fingers dexterously over the wrinkles in the paper. He made an attempt to control his breathing, then gently slipped the note back under his kimono, close to his heart. For even though Noriko had repeated, several times in the note, how much she loved him, Ryu couldn't help but feel that he'd lost her forever. How could he accept her as his wife, knowing that she had bedded down with another man? And the Shogun no less! It was obviously a lie. A horrible, cruel lie, meant to assuage his jealousy and rage by appealing to his patriotic loyalties. Noriko was clever; how could he react at all negatively knowing his wife had been blessed by the beloved Shogun Shitaké? He should be proud of this really. That is what Ryu believed to be his wife's motivation. But Ryu knew better. He would have liked to believe that his lovely Noriko could not be so easily tainted by infidelity unless it were with a man like the Shogun, yet, in reality, she had probably lowered herself for a moment's pleasure with a common farmer. Again, his anger aroused, Ryu took out the note and immediately tore it into little pieces. His chest heaved with his rapid breathing, and he let out a shrill scream as he threw the tiny squares into the air. The wind picked up and began to scatter the papers, and Ryu, in a fit of guilt, began rushing after them, trying to collect the pieces so that he might put them back together. But he could only catch a small number of the pieces; and with a great feeling of loss, Ryu dropped to his knees and began to cry. The salty smell of the nearby sea was caught in the air, promising to preserve this scene in Ryu's memory for the remainder of his life.

Ryu cried for a long while, until he noticed the flickering light of the nearby lighthouse overlooking the cliffs, and his tears ceased flowing as he felt himself caught up in a wave of childhood memory. The lighthouse always overwhelmed him with nostalgic delight. He had been told, sometime in his sixth year, that the lighthouse was built by his great-great grandfather, Kato. He never really believed that to be true, but it always made him feel good to pretend it to be so. The nearby sea recoiled violently against the high cliffs as Ryu began walking toward the lighthouse. As he neared the seemingly ancient structure, he delved even deeper into his fantasies about some sort of a blood connection with it. He placed his hands onto the stone surface and felt the dampness sink into his skin. He wondered if his great-great-grandfather Kato might be seeing him now through the dark mists of the spirit world and be lowering his head in shame. Ryu began to cry, his quiet whimpering blending with the howling of the winds, until he heard a loud thump behind him. Startled, Ryu opened his eyes wide, and hesitated before turning round to see what had caused the noise; finally, with shaking limbs, he turned and let out a ghastly moan.

"Noriko!" he screamed and dropped to his knees at the body of his beloved Noriko, battered and crushed on the rocks after having thrown herself from the top of the lighthouse. The blood escaped her body and settled in pools, mixing with the sprayed water of the broken waves; but her face remained surprisingly untouched. Ryu wrapped his arms around the body and tried to lift it up, but the sickening sound of shattered bones stopped him cold. He leant down and rested his face against hers, and stroked her mouth, smearing her lips with the moss that covered his hands after placing them on the lighthouse.

"Noriko," he cried. "I forgive you."

Lord Shitaké Ozamu became Shogun at the age of eight, his father having fallen at the battle of Bizen while warring against the Migi: dying, as he had lived, gloriously. It took the Migi bowmen no less than thirty-three arrows at close range to extinguish that extraordinary life. It was a rare moment indeed that Lord Shitaké's thoughts did not fall on the memory of his father's death. It seemed almost a curse; especially in the days of damnable peace he now lived; for all hopes of an equally honorable death were little but dreams.

However, Lord Shitaké's thoughts were far removed from his father's glory as he rolled the soft, naked body of the girl Chikako off him after loudly reaching climax. The air rushed out of the goose down pillows as the two bodies relaxed, and

Lord Shitaké began stroking the silky skin of Chikako's sweat beaded stomach, watching it heave with her heavy breaths.

"An origami contest, you say. What a strange fancy," Lord Shitaké said between gasps for air.

5

Kimitaké Oin waded through the gray fog like a lost ship. He had entered Kaicho Swamp with his path well illumined by the light of the full moon, but the fog came quickly, and his way was now lost. The sharp swamp weeds brushed against his padded feet, making soft scraping sounds as the rough stems caught on the cloth with each step he took. Normally on guard for any attack that might come, Kimitaké relaxed the grip on his sword, sure he would hear any approaching enemy; for no matter how lightly he stepped, the thick, trudging splash of the swampy water echoed in the distance, seeming to collide and recoil against the heavy wall of fog. A toad's croak could be heard, loudly, as if unaffected by the fog; and Kimitaké lowered his head, trying to catch a glimpse of it, feeling a bit childish as he did so.

He wrapped his cloak tightly around him as the wind picked up, sending a chill into the air, and his heart quickened slightly as he heard a muted splash not too far behind him. Once more, his fingers curled around the handle of his sword and, silent but for a metallic hiss, he began to slide it from its sheath.

"It could be the toad," he thought, and not long afterward, a responsive croak served to calm him again. With his sword still halfway out of the sheath, Kimitaké smiled and harrumphed good-heartedly. But as he began to walk again, he couldn't help but feel a strong presence weighing down on him; the feeling of repentance not earned, and guilt from an unknown cause. He slid the sword back into the sheath, but nonetheless held tightly onto it, tapping the edge of the handle with his free hand. He was sure he was not being followed, so why did he feel so endangered?

"Whoever it is could be standing still," he thought. "I could be walking right toward him."

Suddenly, Kimitaké froze, and quickly pulled his sword fully from its sheath as he saw plainly the dark silhouetted figure of a man but five feet away from him. He held his sword high in a defensive position, and the fog seemed to break for an instant, allowing the moonlight to glint off the blade. But the fog reformed, and the moon's shiny glint slowly melted along the length of the blade until it was lost again. Kimitaké breathed calmly, waiting for the attack. He stretched out his front foot and splashed it quickly in the water, hoping to goad his unseen enemy, but still no attack. He kept his stance until he could no longer count the seconds until, strangely, he began to feel a certain loss of time. He began to feel that he had been lost in the swamp, in the fog, waiting for the attack of an unseen enemy not for days, but for years, ages. And then, in an instant, the air filled with the clamorous noise of the croaking of a thousand toads. The sound came unbearably to Kimitaké's ears, and fear began to enter his heart for the first time. But no matter how unbearable, Kimitaké would not break his stance to cover his ears, even when the blood began to flow from them. His kept the stance, frozen in place and time, his whole being beginning to shake; until, just as suddenly as it started, the noise ceased.

Kimitaké let out a gasp and turned his head to the left and right, trying desperately to see through the fog, when a deep, hollow voice was heard.

"I am usually without witness," the voice said, and Kimitaké turned in circles, unable to focus on which direction the speaker lay. Once more, he raised his sword high.

"Who are you?" he asked in a tone of defiance.

"Toyama Shōki," came the voice, and Kimitaké jumped back as he found himself face to face with

21

a tall, dark figure, dressed all in white but covered by a pitch-black shroud, his face hidden in shadow by a large-brimmed woven straw hat. Kimitaké tried to compose himself, noticing firstly that this man, Toyama Shōki, had his hands safely away from his sword belt.

"Are you lost in the swamp?" the figure asked. Kimitaké could not take his eyes off the man, and so stared, feeling more curiosity than aggression.

"What are you doing here?" he asked.

"I was looking for something," said the figure.

"Have you found what you were looking for?" asked Kimitaké, questioning if it were not he the figure was searching for.

"Some of them," the figure answered, what little of his face peered out from the shadows showing no emotion. It was not lost on Kimitaké that the fog seemed to be drifting closer, flowing, and seeming to make shapes in the air.

"What Lord do you serve?" he asked.

"I serve no lord," answered the man. Kimitaké felt the grip on his sword loosening.

"Are you Ronin?" he asked, beginning to feel a deep connection with this Toyama Shōki, though he knew not why.

"I serve only her," Toyama answered, pointing his finger in the air. Kimitaké followed the pointing finger, lifting his head to the sky, and was suddenly blinded by sunlight. He gave a pained cry and flung his arm over his face to cover his eyes. His legs gave out as if the full weight of the sun were pressing down on him, and he fell full-bodied into the swamp. He lay face down in the swamp for a moment, then rose and took a breath. The swampy water dripped from his kimono as he stood, giving the sound of a light spring shower. He looked around and saw the ends of the swamp not twenty yards ahead, and a small farm nearby. Strangely, Kimitaké did not wonder about the fog; he did not wonder about the time, or how day had come so quickly from night. He wondered only about Toyama Shōki; and began to feel, at last, that he had found a rival worthy of the name. Kimitaké Oin stood straight and began walking toward the farm at the edge of Kaicho Swamp.

6

Jacobin Endo was born in the far north of the country, or rather, Todogatsu Island off the southern tip of Hokkaido; and born to a Christian household. Having been reared on the doctrines of the Christian faith, it is not surprising that Endo, at a very early age, rebelled against his family and became a bloody activist against the Church and, more specifically, against Western encroachment of the land altogether. But having the first name Jacobin makes for a peculiar anti-Christian bandit and, though he did at some time in his youth make attempts at a pseudonym, the others in his acquaintance always seemed to enjoy calling him by his Christian name. Even those who had never met him before referred to him by this name; and so, it came to be more of a nickname than a given name. Thus, Jacobinin continued, however reluctantly, to go by that name. Be that as it may; at some point, Jacobin Endo had a re-awakening, and chose once again to follow the faith of his Father and Mother; though it should be said he chose the Dutch over the Spanish church. A number of reasons could be given for this turnaround, but the most correct would probably be the reason given by one Miyashi Tetsuo, a onetime friend of Endo's who observed, while in a drunken state, "Old Jacobin ran off to join the Holy Father's because it gave him an excuse to cause bloodshed." And this is true, as Endo's violence had not in any way decreased since taking up the burden; he had even been known to mutilate a young child beyond all repair who, in a casual mistake of pronunciation, accidentally referred to the Almighty God as "impotent", rather than "omnipotent".

Jacobin Endo was sitting in the Ariyoshi Tavern, drinking sake, when a pitiful sight caught his eyes. What he saw was Hojo Ryu, slumped in the corner and drowning in his own wretchedness. Endo smiled and began to rub the crucifix hanging by his chest, and was very pleased that this moment might come along so that he might be able to perform for the others in the tavern his ability to give charity, and at such an opportune moment, before he had drunk too much.

Jacobin Endo stood up and brushed his robes

behind him, then walked slowly and confidently up to Hojo Ryu and, without asking, knelt before the grief-stricken man.

"Is there anything I can--?"

"Saké!" yelled Hojo, paying no attention to Endo.

"Here, you may finish mine," said Endo, handing over his saucer. Hojo stared at the saucer as if unsure what to do, then snatched it away and gulped the sake down.

"Sakeeeeeé!!!" Hojo screamed hoarsely and bounced the wooden saucer on the floor. It rolled across the tavern floor, then with a dull thud, hit the wall and began to spin like a top.

"I tell you to shut him up," said the owner of the tavern, hobbling over to the two men as fast as his elderly frame would carry him. "He is disturbing my customers!"

"Please," said Endo, holding up his hand as a sign of peace. "I will calm him, but can't you see this man is in pain? It will take time, maybe all night, but that is a small price to pay for the salvation of his very soul, don't you think?"

The owner crossed his eyes in confusion and looked at the two men, finally throwing his hands into the air and walking off. Endo then leaned in close, practically touching noses with the drunken Hojo.

"If you would like to talk, I am here to listen," he said in a sympathetic tone. Hojo seemed to make an honest attempt to look into Endo's eyes, but was unable to, and instead, nodded his head as if it were only precariously attached to his body.

"Boiled fish," he said, slurring his words.

"You want boiled fish?" asked Endo. "Wouldn't you rather have some absolution first?"

Just then, the door to the tavern was pushed open as if by a large gust of wind; but when Endo, and even Hojo, turned to look, all they saw was a robust farmer standing at the entrance.

"Ah, good evening, Kita," yelled the owner of the tavern from across the room. "What can I get for you?"

"Tea," said the man, his voice deep and stern, quite unlike that usually thought of as a farmer's. Endo noticed the man holding a stack of leaflets.

"Tea?" asked the owner in surprise, "no saké?"

"No saké tonight," answered the farmer. "Tonight is not a night for drink. Have you seen these?" he asked the owner, holding out the leaflets. "Just tonight, I saw several horsemen come from Lord Shitaké's Castle. Four of them. One rode to the south, and the others, north, west and east. They are all carrying these and throwing them about."

"Well then, let's have a look," said the owner,

his curiosity piqued. He grabbed one of the leaflets from Kita and held it close to his face. "Ah, how strange," he exclaimed.

"Well? What is it then?" asked several farmers who had been sitting huddled in the corner. Endo had not noticed them before, but now they seemed to come alive, as if appearing from nowhere. They spoke loudly and belligerently, demanding to know what the leaflets said. The owner held up his hands to quiet them, but the large farmer, Kita, seemed to tire of their voices.

"Silence!" he screamed. The farmers quieted down, and Endo himself felt the need to shut up, even though he had not spoken a word in minutes.

"I will tell you what they say," said Kita. "The Lord Shitaké is going to hold a contest. An origami contest!" After hearing this, a harsh gasp escaped from the mouths of all the patrons in the tavern, except for Endo.

"Why does the news of an origami contest frighten them so?" he asked the drunken Hojo, but Hojo merely sneered.

"You all know what that means don't you?" continued Kita, and the patrons all knelt their heads in unison.

"Tiki Kōji!" said the owner of the tavern, his hushed voice filled with dread.

"That's right," said Kita, slamming the leaflets

onto the ground. "Thanks to these leaflets, Tiki Kōji is sure to return!"

The patrons grew even more silent; then one by one they stood up, and no matter how much they had drunk throughout the night, all walked soberly out of the tavern and disappeared in the night. Endo watched in curiosity through dark narrow eyes, until he looked down and marveled that he had been rubbing his crucifix the entire time. He took a breath and tucked the crucifix into his robes before turning once more to Hojo who, of all the patrons, remained in the tavern.

"Who is this Tiki Kōji?" he asked. Hojo did not answer; he merely lowered his head and stared at the floor with sleepy eyes. Endo waited for an answer, but sensing he was not going to get one he stood up, and, taking a few bills from his robes, placed them at the feet of Hojo before turning to leave. But as he reached the exit and prepared to walk out of the tavern, he heard the slurred voice of Hojo.

"The Lord Shitaké…has…fathered an illegitimate child," he said. Kendo's eyes widened and he quickly turned round to face Hojo.

"What was that?" he asked.

"The Lord Shitaké," continued Hojo, speaking so slowly that his voice seemed not his own but that of some spirit or demon talking through a reanimated corpse. "The Lord Shitaké has fathered an illegitimate child. A son."

"A son?" Endo gasped, and sat back down next to Hojo. "Tell me," he said softly, "tell me what you know of this…son."

Tiki Kōji had deflowered his fair share of virgins in his lifetime, though *fair share* wouldn't be the way he would describe it. In its own way, this is an explanation for the three dead men lying at his feet, the three men being the father and two brothers of the twelve-year-old girl Kōji had had his way with two nights before. They had come seeking justice; alas, none was found.

Kōji paced the bodies until a fine ovular track was made around them from his bare-footed steps, and quietly folded a piece of green rice paper into the shape of a leaping tiger. Gently, he placed this at the foot of the first victim, the eldest of the two brothers. He then, in turn, folded a snowflake from a cream-colored paper and placed this at the foot of the youngest brother; and a red papered dragon placed at the foot of the father. He then stared down at his victims, and a faint smile echoed through the look of pity on his face as he admired his handiwork; not so much the killing, which took masterful strokes from his kitana, but the origami. It was always something he took great pride in, and there was not a single shape known to man that he could not fold. In fact, Tiki Kōji could not remember a time he had ever needed to practice; it just seemed a natural inclination of his to be able to fold paper, and always perfectly. It was much the same way with his swordsmanship. In this he was master as well. This might be an explanation for his seemingly reckless ways and the ease with which he allowed himself to demonstrate his skills, the consequences of which were deaths that could be numbered in the thousands. He was afraid of nothing, because nobody had ever posed a challenge to him. It was for this reason that Shogun Shitaké merely exiled him after he had gone on a rampage through the villages surrounding the castle, instead of having him assassinated; for the Shogun knew that no man would be able to kill Tiki Kōji, so why take the risk of inciting his wrath when he could simply take advantage of Kōji's honorable ways and send him off, knowing that he would respect the wishes of his Lord and disappear.

And so Kōji had wandered the country as a

Ronin for the last five years, never once having stepped foot into the lands of Shitaké. In those five years, he had been hard at work, between killings, penning his autobiography, a great section of this being his reflections on the great and mysterious art of origami. But recently Kōji had grown anxious. He was coming to the end of his narrative, but could see no proper ending in sight. He loathed the idea of having to finish his great work with a simple '…I grew old and withered.' What he needed was a grand finale, something that would insure his place in the future lore of the country. It was something he had begun to fear he would never have, until the day he found a certain leaflet.

It was on the same night he had deflowered the twelve-year-old girl that he found the leaflet. He caught sight of it as it was blowing in the wind and, somewhat giddily chased it down. Kōji had always been good at entertaining himself, and chasing the leaflet was a suitable exercise, no matter how silly. He finally caught up with the leaflet when the wind trapped it between the forking limbs of a poplar tree. When he read the announcement of the origami contest at Shitaké's palace, it seemed to him to be a gift from the gods. Surely Lord Shitaké was aware that he would find one of those leaflets, and Kōji wondered if this were not some secret summons. Perhaps Lord Shitaké was in some sort of trouble, or perhaps he was a fool and had decided after five years that a trap must be sprung so that he might finally be rid of the specter that was Tiki Kōji. Either way would be good enough for him; and so Kōji smiled as he re-read the pamphlet, over and over again, sitting comfortably next to the three dead bodies. Suddenly thought occurred to him, and he took out a small ledger book bound with silken string and, opening it, he scribed these words at the top of a page nearing the end of the book: "*About the Lord Shitaké, and the contest of folded paper.*"

Lady Keiko had been practicing more than ever after the announcement of the contest, and she was coming ever closer to that perfect crane, preferring to use the golden paper even though it was the hardest to acquire. But her mistakes were few and far between now, so she felt the waste less risky. As well as nearly mastering the crane, she sat surrounded by piles of lotus blossoms, frogs, and boxes requiring several different colors of paper. She finished folding another crane and was in the midst of admiring herself when the Shogun entered her quarters; having no beaded pillows at hand, she covered up the piles of paper with her kimono, risking Lord Shitaké's ill favor of her unkempt appearance over his finding her at work on origami.

"Keiko," said Lord Shitaké, looking exactly as

he looked in the portrait of him hanging over the halls of the court. "It is time for bed, quit whatever it is you are doing and come." Lady Keiko nodded respectfully and Lord Shitaké exited the room. She then collected all of the papers and hid them under the mats on the floor before leaving the room herself and retiring to the sleeping chambers.

Once in bed, Lady Keiko was surprised to catch the scent of the girl Chikako, and she looked over at her husband with a look of disgust, the room being too dark for him to see it even if he were not sleeping so soundly. The disgust was not from the reminder that her husband had bedded down with the girl, but rather the fact that he had refused to wash the bed's coverings. But this disgust, too, seemed to fade away as she was next reminded how it was her will that Chikako sleep with Lord Shitaké and, thinking on the contest that act had won her, she suddenly found the scent very sweet, and a small part of her wished it were Chikako she now lay next to rather than her husband. But her thoughts, making her so active, served to wake the Shogun, and Lady Keiko quickly shut her eyes to feign sleep.

"Keiko," said Lord Shitaké. "Keiko, I yearn. Wake up." Lady Keiko opened her eyes drowsily and smiled.

"What is it now my Lord?" she asked naively.

"My passion is great," said Lord Shitaké, uncovering his wife's breasts and rubbing his hands up and down the length of her body. Lady Keiko continued to smile and moaned slightly at her husband's touch, when suddenly a vision crossed her mind. In an instant, her inner sight was filled with geometric patterns and integrated shapes, and almost by instinct she knew this pattern to be the secret behind the perfect crane. Quickly, she climbed away from her husband and out of the bed.

"Excuse me please," she said. "There is something I must see to, an urgent matter, I beg your pardon." And with this, she bowed, and left the room, only half covered with a sheet, determined to fold the crane that night.

Lord Shitaké stared in utter surprise and disbelief as his wife left the room, his passion unfulfilled.

"Keiko!" he yelled and waited for her return. But when she did not return in the short seconds he felt were sufficient, he began to grow angry, frustrated.

"Keiko!" he yelled again.

9

Kimitaké Oin twirled his sandals around his right index finger as he sat basking in the sun, listening to the calming waters of a clear stream, his eyes focused on the hundreds of loose pebbles refusing to move under the water's torrent. An old man played a soothing rokudan not too far off, but distant enough to be out of sight. As always, Oin pondered the meaning of life, particularly his own, and how best society could benefit from his existence, until he witnessed a small dog approaching. The dog had apparently been very well treated thus far by men, for it trotted up to Oin and greedily pushed its muzzle under his armpit. It sat still as Oin scratched between its ears, and, in its pleasure, the sound of its panting began to overpower those of the stream and the koto. Oin smiled and knelt down to scratch the dog's chest when a small child, a young boy of about eight years, appeared searching for the dog. The boy looked to the left and to the right, but his eyes scanned directly past Oin, apparently under the assumption the dog would never cavort with a stranger. Oin watched the boy for several seconds, finding amazement in the anxiety the boy felt for the wellbeing of his animal.

"Over here boy," he said at last. The dog sat still as the boy walked over, stopping within fifteen feet of Oin, not wanting to get too close, and patted his leg. The dog looked up at Oin, and Oin motioned with his eyes that it was proper for it to obey the boy's summons. The dog then ran gleefully to the boy who quickly began to scold it. Oin's eyes saddened as he watched the animal tuck its tail between its legs and follow the boy to wherever they had come from. They were soon lost from view due to an overgrowth of cedar trees that had once been part of a great forest, but which was now little more than a small wood. If one were to paint the small section of overgrowth, one could give the impression that the rest of the forest was still there, teeming with life; and Oin himself had observed several of the locals covering one or other of their eyes as they approached the overgrowth while walking along the small path to the nearest town; using this trick to, as he guessed, picture in their minds the forest as it once was. A legend had sprung up over this dead wood. Apparently, this was the forest whose trees were used in the building of defenses at the time of the Mongol invasion, and, under this notion, one could not see in the clearing a sad reminder of the wasting of nature, but of a noble sacrifice; earth, and later, wind, coming together for the survival of the Japanese people. The people had not even given it a name, for fear of that being a sign of disrespect, for how can you name something that has created you?

Kimitaké Oin sighed, and his thoughts became lost in his memory of Toyama Shōki. But still, he did not think of the strangeness of that night in the swamp, or of the circumstances by which he met up with the shrouded man; he thought only of one thing: how much he would like to fight him. Kimitaké Oin wanted that very much. And if he lost, he would like, then, to be buried at this clearing, at the edge of the overgrowth.

He stayed in that place until nightfall, thinking of Toyama Shōki trying to piece together a face by which he might recognize the man. The moon, rising high overhead, created wicked shadows out of the nearby foliage, but Oin was unafraid. The crickets began to chirp; the wind began to howl; the remaining cedars of the once great forest rustled against one another; still, Oin was unafraid. Oin diverted his thoughts away from Toyama Shōki and onto the sickness of the world. Were the sounds of nature a lament for humankind? Or was it laughter? The deep, terrible laughter that only a being as old as the Earth could be capable of?

Just then he awoke; unaware, even, that he had fallen asleep; and was surprised to see the dog from earlier in the day sleeping soundly next to him, curled up in a little ball. Oin looked down at the dog, placed his hand on its head, and was afraid. It was then, that the deep hollow voice of Toyama Shōki spoke out from the shadows.

"What is best in man?" was the question asked, and Oin jumped to his feet, pulling out his sword. The dog remained lost in sleep.

"It is him!" exclaimed Oin. The firm figure of Shōki could be seen standing in the middle of the overgrowth, though covered in shadows.

"What is best in man?" Shōki asked again. Oin held out his blade as a challenge, but Shōki remained amongst the trees.

"Why do you ask me this?" Oin asked, feeling his muscles tense with anticipation.

"Why do you not answer?" came the reply, though the tone was not that of a question asked, but of a firm accusation.

"Honor," said Oin, hoping that an answer would start the fight.

"Wrong," responded Shōki without a movement.

"Loyalty."

"Wrong."

"Sacrifice," said Oin, with passion in his voice, and he waited for Shōki's response.

"Wrong," said Shōki, his voice even deeper than before; and Oin caught, like a haunting demon reaching out from the void, the sharp gleam of Toyama Shōki's sword as it was slowly pulled from its sheath, as if the shadows themselves could not penetrate the blade. The blade made a heavy sound, as if it were twice the weight of a normal sword, and Oin wondered if it might not be foreign made; but he soon lost all thought as his mind and body became one, ready for the fight. He lifted his sword high as Toyama Shōki began to move toward him, the twigs and underbrush snapping loudly with every step. His body slowly left the shadows and came out into the light of the moon. At first, it appeared to Oin that Shōki was armored, but this must have been a trick of the light for, as Shōki moved ever closer, he saw plainly that the man was dressed exactly as before; all in white but with a dark shroud and the woven straw hat.

"Discipline," Oin shouted out suddenly, quite

42

without thinking, and Shōki stopped.

"Yes," said Shōki, his voice low and rumbling like the forewarnings of an earthquake. He then began to walk toward Oin once more, his sword still drawn. Oin raised his sword higher and gulped.

"Discipline…what made you choose this? Out of all that is in man," asked Shōki, moving closer.

"Because I witness you, and I am afraid. But you are what I have been searching for, so I must stand and fight you. This is discipline, my discipline. I fear you and, dare I say it, a part of me wishes not to fight you; but knowing that I must fight you, I must stand my ground," Oin responded.

"And in this you find pleasure," stated Shōki, and Oin could see a slight smile stretch across that formless face. Oin did not answer. "The dog, is it yours?"

"No," Oin answered, feeling very confused.

"A dog is a disciplined animal. The dog receives a lot of scorn for his willingness to obey. Some prefer cats, because they are so headstrong and willful, but a dog is disciplined. It does not like to do simple little tricks that argue with its dignity; it does not enjoy the act itself. What the dog enjoys is knowing that, no matter how much he dislikes following a command, he has the discipline to do just that, no matter what pain it may bring him. The dog does not truly follow commands; it merely exercises its will, and its scorn for man. The knowledge that it may endure the pain, and the humiliation, by an act of its own will. That knowledge is what is best in man."

"Who are you?" Oin asked desperately. "I must know." Shōki twirled his sword in the air, cutting the wind, and placed it back in its sheath.

"Journey to the west," he said. "It is there you will find your rival."

Jacobin Endo entered the palace with very little trouble. It didn't hurt that his spiritual father, Xavier Takei, was a confidant of the Shogun. Lord Shitaké had been good to the Christian community in his realm, though for unknown reasons, and Endo felt it absolutely necessary that he know about this illegitimate child. A son, even an illegitimate son, would have claims to the Shogunate; and illegitimate children have a certain tendency to follow the exact opposite course of their fathers. Endo was not about to allow the already precarious position of the Christian community to fall into any more uncertainties.

Xavier Takei welcomed Endo with a low bow, his hands held together, and led him to an empty room, plain but for a black rectangular cushion at the far end. In this room Endo waited. The sun shone through the wooden paneling of the walls and through these panels could be seen the outer edges of the palace gardens. Endo sat still, his legs crossed, and contemplated his God while the wind blew through the bamboo, brushing it against the outside walls of the room. The sound from the wind blowing through the gardens was intermingled with that of a troop of Lord Shitaké's warriors leaving the castle grounds on horseback. Their armor clattered with the bustling of the horses, and a powerful voice shouted commands as the earth seemed to shake with the strength of the horse's hooves. Endo wrapped his fingers around his crucifix and trembled. Moments later, Xavier Takei returned and introduced Lord Shitaké.

The Shogun entered the room without a word, followed by three of his retainers, and sat down on the cushion at the far end of the room. He was dressed for riding, and sat cross legged with his hands placed on his hip while his three retainers were armored. Xavier Takei sat meekly on his knees before the Shogun, bowing repeatedly as he introduced, with apologies, Jacobin Endo. Endo suddenly felt overcome with disgust as he witnessed with what feebleness his spiritual father acted in the presence of the Shogun; he had always had such a stern, glorious manner while preaching to the converts; but now he was nothing more than an old man.

"Jacobin," said Takei, smiling pitifully, "please tell the Lord why you have come to see him. We have interrupted his hunting party, you see." Endo increased the pressure of his fingers as they rubbed the crucifix, and stared at the Shogun and his men before speaking.

"I have come to warn the Noble Lord of a grave matter," he said, bowing. "And though I know the Lord is aware of all that happens in his realm, I fear that there is one thing he has--overlooked." Lord Shitaké's eyes narrowed in a mixture of anger and confusion. Should he be insulted, or should he be curious as to what this Christian was speaking about? Endo risked much. He would have preferred a private audience with the Shogun, for fear of damaging his prestige in front of his men, but this was as close as he was going to get. "I fear--that the Shogun has sired a child, a son, with a common woman. I do not know how often the Lord partakes in these affairs, perhaps this was only one time; and so, perhaps also, you might remember her all the more; but this woman, whose name was--what was it? Ah, Hojo Noriko--" Lord Shitaké's eyes widened, and this did not go unnoticed by Endo, who now spoke with more confidence. "The woman, Noriko, now deceased, gave birth to a baby boy on this same day, seven years ago."

The Shogun's retainers looked down at him; a slight fear could be read in their features. The Shogun meanwhile had regained his composure. He sat up straight and cleared his throat.

"How is it you know this?" he asked.

"I have met with the boy's father--excuse me, the man who until several days ago believed himself to be the father. He was quite a drunkard, Lord; and, I dare say, I would not trust this man to raise this child."

"What is your meaning? Do you suggest that I accept this child, and make my affairs known to the public? Do you think me such a fool?"

"Not at all Lord; I beg your pardon for any misunderstanding. What I mean to say is, in light of the threat this boy might one day become, I would not--suffer the boy to live. It is in your best interests, Lord," said Endo, bowing once more. As he lowered his head, he caught sight of Takei who now stared at him, a look of shock and utter disbelief on his face.

"Jacobin--" he began, his voice shaking and breathless, but Lord Shitaké interrupted.

"Very well," he said sternly. "Tell me where the boy is and, also, the drunkard of a father."

"Again, I apologize, Lord," said Endo. "I am

not too familiar with your lands, and I am afraid I have only seen the boy once. After Hojo told me his story, I followed him home, quite without his knowing it, and saw him with the boy only then. But it looked as if the man were taking him away. They went in an easterly direction. I know not for how long, or even how far they got. I came here immediately after seeing this."

Lord Shitaké sighed deeply and then looked down at the shaking Xavier Takei.

"What do you suggest Takei? You who would consider yourself my councilor." Takei gave no answer, as if the fear of what he knew must happen had already scarred him beyond all belief, robbing him of his free will, and making him into a cowering heap. Lord Shitaké laughed softly. "What is it your scriptures say?" And after saying this, he laughed again, loudly.

Endo kept his eyes on the floor, rubbing his crucifix. A long strand of hair fell into his face, and he looked closely at it. Lord Shitaké turned to his retainers.

"Find the boy and kill him," he ordered. "And if you have any trouble, kill every son born on this day, seven years ago." He then turned to Endo. "You may leave, and give thanks to your Jesus that I have done him yet another favor in Japan."

Endo stood up and bowed, then exited the room;

but before he left the palace, he walked around to the gardens and knelt between the bamboo stalks. Moments afterward, the Shogun left the castle with his retainers, and Endo heard later that night he had successfully trapped and killed several foxes.

11

Tiki Kōji reached the outer lands of Lord Shitaké in very short time and, feeling all the less impatient to arrive at the castle--knowing that it would be no more than two days ride-he dismounted his horse and had a bath in a nearby stream. Afterward he sat down to a meal of freshly caught fish and a small basket of oranges stolen from a nearby orchard. The owner of the orchard, an elderly widow of sixty- eight years, inspired Kōji to laughter as she chased him down with all the spryness of a young woman; and, as he sat at the bank of the stream biting into the fruit, he became sexually aroused, imagining the old woman as she might have looked in her youth. He almost regretted running away from her, as a closer inspection of her features would have made his fantasies all the more detailed.

After eating the meal, Kōji washed his hands in the stream, took his ledger book from his saddle bag and, sitting down comfortably against a small boulder, he began to read through it, as always, amazed by his own thoughts.

On the art of Origami, the founding and the passing on of:

The Origami, or the folded paper, comes to us as a gift of Amaterasu, the sun goddess, but its progenitor on this earth was one Wei-Lei Ping, a Chinese aristocrat from the South of that country. It is said that Wei-Lei Ping discovered the art of the folded paper as a means with which to communicate with the Bodhisattva, as a careful alternative to meditation and prayer. It is also said that Wei-Lei Ping, having entered into the misty lands after much strong concentration, was told by the Buddha that his excellence in the art of the folded paper showed him to be a man whose soul was ill-kept and over-passionate, and thus too desirous of the joys of life to reach Nirvana; and Wei-Lei Ping, being fearful of repeating the cycle of life on this earth, quickly came upon a plan with which to rid himself of the art. But the folded paper, having become so much a part of his life, was not something so easily discarded. It had become dear to him, and even though it might be a risk to his soul, he could not simply stop the art he felt he had created. So in the ways of so many aristocratic inventors, Wei-Lei Ping merely decided to pass the art down to another after it had served its purpose to himself. He would be free of the desire in his soul, that desire being to perfect the art and, also, the art would be able to live on, to further flower and evolve, here on this earth, while he himself would have long since joined with the Buddha in everlasting nothingness.

The man he found to pass the art onto, was a Buddhist monk from these lands, Japanese of common birth but of noble heart, named Tenchi Go-Jirro. Go-Jirro was carried across the sea in his youth by his grandmother, who was determined to see him grow to be a fine priest. Go-Jirro is said to have hated the mainland passionately, and his hatred of the Chinese people and ways was only somewhat less remarkable; while in this land, he carried within him, a memory of the shrine of Hiroki, a Shinto shrine that stood upon a hill overlooking his boyhood home. He longed for the day he would return, and counted the moments until then. But then, while studying at the Buddhist temple, he met Wei-Lei Ping.

Wei-Lei Ping paid special attention to the young boy from Japan, and found in him the reliever of his burden. Wei-Lei Ping took the boy under his wing. It should not be supposed that Go-Jirro was any happier with Wei-Lei Ping than with the other Chinese, but Wei-Lei Ping was patient, as are all of his race, and nurtured the boy well, so that, after many years, Go-Jirro could say he felt for the man a certain respect, if not love. Many years passed, until Go-Jirro's nineteenth birthday; the day he informed his tutor that he intended to return to Japan as soon as the weather permitted the voyage. Wei-Lei Ping felt a heaviness in his heart for he had learned to love the boy, if for no other reason than he saw in him a way for his soul to reach the next world. And so, feeling his time begin to shorten, Wei-Lei Ping finally began to teach young Go-Jirro the art of the folded paper.

It took many years for Go-Jirro to capture even the rudiments of the art, but with much practice, coupled with the patient teachings of Wei-Lei, Go-Jirro soon became a master, second only to his teacher. It is said that at this time, Go-Jirro developed a love for the mainland and, in particular, its folkways; and, in fact, delayed his journey home by two decades. It was on his thirty-ninth birthday that Go-Jirro finally set sail for his return to Japan. It was the day after the death of Wei-Lei Ping, on which Go-Jirro sat at his bedside, gently praying for the soul of his beloved teacher. And so Tenchi Go-Jirro was on his way home, back *to the land of his memories, well versed not only in the art of paper folding that he had since named Origami, but also in the art of calligraphy and many other aristocratic Chinese arts. Go-Jirro watched the stars on that voyage, and was at peace until, as it is recorded in his journals written many years later, he was visited by the ghost of Wei-Lei Ping. The spectral image of his master mixed with the rolling currents of the sea as it floated above deck, looking down at the quivering Go-Jirro, and the briny smell of the water seemed a representation of the cursed soul itself.*

"Why do you haunt me in this way?" Go-Jirro asked the ghost.

"I am doomed," replied the ghost, mournfully, and raising its hands to its ears as if to shut out some dreadful noise unheard on this earthly realm. "My soul is trapped here in the void, unable to enter into Nirvana. You must help me."

"What can I do to help, Master?" asked Go-Jirro.

"I waited too long in my pride to teach you the art of folded paper," said the ghost. "And so I am to be punished for my delay, doomed to float in this nothingness between two worlds, until the day of the perfect fold. The one fold I never taught you, and am still unable to teach. You must find this fold, discover its secret, and once it is done, the

Buddha himself will be the judge; in this only is my salvation. Discover the golden lotus Go-Jirro. Free my soul."

With this did the ghost of Wei-Lei Ping depart from the eyes of Tenchi Go-Jirro. And Go-Jirro swore from that day on that he would discover the secret fold in which he would free the soul of his teacher. But the fold was never discovered. Go-Jirro passed the origami to his first daughter, Ochikubo; and she, in turn, to her first daughter, and so on, in the hopes that one day the fold would be made; until the origami found its way into the houses of the nobles, only to become a leisurely past-time for children and courtiers. The Golden Lotus remains a mystery, and Wei-Lei Ping's soul is forever trapped between the two worlds until the day of its discovery.

Tiki Kōji closed the book and sighed, knowing in his heart that he would be the one to discover the secret fold of the Golden Lotus.

12

Kimitaké Oin had been traveling west for five days when he reached the village of Saikako, and strange thoughts occurred to him after finding all the villagers were shut up in their homes. The sun began to lower and Oin wrapped his kimono tightly around him as the wind began to chill. He quickened his pace, knowing it would be more difficult to find lodgings once nightfall had set in. Walking through the village, Oin kept an eye out for an inn but, out of the three he found, no rooms were available. And so, consoling himself to the fact another night was to be spent under the stars, he began to walk more leisurely and, as he passed the ramshackle houses lining the dirt road, he admired the o-fuda pasted onto the doors. Although most were the usual Sutras, Oin couldn't help feeling that there was an unusual amount of fear to them, as if the villagers really believed there to be goblins about. The more he paid attention, the more he realized the amount of o-fuda upon the doors. It was not unusual to see several houses in a village decorated with them, especially if there were newborn children about; but the houses of Saikako were littered with them, and the air was filled with their rustling, like dry leaves fallen from the trees blowing in the wind.

Oin began to fear himself after reading enough of the holy charms, and was suddenly filled with a great hope. Perhaps he was on the right track after all. Toyama Shōki had told him he would find his rival in the west, and Oin knew what this meant. Shōki had felt his fear and had not wanted to spoil the fight because of it; and so, out of respect, he had given Oin a chance to find his courage, until the day they would meet again. Oin turned in a circle, taking in a view of the entire village and thought, "Such a fearful place. Who could lie in such fear but you Shōki?" And then Oin at last caught sight of a villager. It was an older man, dressed in rags and pushing a wheelbarrow down the street, about thirty yards from where Oin stood. The man was plainly seen in the moonlight and Oin slowly stepped into the middle of the road to make himself visible to the man. The man continued to approach him, head down, eyes only directly ahead of him on the road, until, when he had come a little closer, Oin cleared his throat to announce his presence. The man looked up with a start and, with a short cry, he quickly jumped off the road and hid behind a house. Oin stared in curiosity as the man slowly poked his head out from behind the house; then, apparently finding nothing to fear, he came back out, returning to his wheelbarrow, continuing on his way down the road. Oin stood still as the man passed, and managed, through a great strength of discipline, not to ask the man what had frightened him so. He continued to watch the old man, now walking away from him, until a noise was heard behind him. Turning, Oin saw a small boy peeking out from one of the windows of the house the old man had hidden behind. The boy looked over at Oin, then lowered his head back into the house. Oin, now more curious than ever, walked toward the house and, stopping at its door, read the o-fuda before knocking. It was a strange charm for the Western lands, a dharani, a magical text. Oin then prepared to knock, but before doing so, the door was suddenly opened. Looking down, Oin saw the boy.

"My apologies," said Oin, "could you fetch your father for me boy?" The boy looked up at Oin with a strange and unnatural maturity shining in his eyes, and then, without a word, he left, returning moments later with his father, who was Hojo Ryu.

"What do you want?" Hojo asked belligerently, looking down at Oin's sword, and Oin found he was at a loss for words, not understanding himself why he had entered into that house.

"It is a strange night," he responded slowly, trying to grasp at words in the air. "I wonder why this village is so guarded; can you tell me?" Hojo continued to stare at the sword, but then turned toward his son.

"Go into the other room Kauro," he said, and the boy left the room. Hojo then sat down in front of Oin, his legs crossed. Oin waited a moment in silence before kneeling down across from him. "This village is cursed with a violent memory," Hojo began. "And it fears a return to the dark times."

"Dark times? But this land has been peaceful for quite some time. I hear Lord Shitaké has a great care for the people."

At the sound of Shitaké's name, Hojo's body grew tense, and he answered: "They await a man who has no scruples and who does not think twice before killing man, woman, or child. They hope to remain hidden from him through mundane activities."

Oin began to grow uncomfortable.

"I wonder if you have seen a man," he said, and took out a piece of paper with a rough drawing of a man resembling Toyama Shōki. "I have been looking for him; he might have passed through a short time ago." Hojo took the paper and studied the portrait, staring long and hard at it. It seemed to have a mesmerizing effect on him.

"What strange eyes," he said under his breath. Then, almost as if he were forcing himself, he handed the paper back to Oin. "I have never seen a man such as this. I fear if I were to, I would remember those eyes until my dying day. However, by your drawing, the man looks to be some sort of a student, and there is a school inside the castle walls. He may have gone straight there. It is easy to bypass this village on the way." Oin put the paper away feeling a certain despair.

"Is it far to the Shogun's castle?" he asked. Hojo was silent for a moment before answering.

"It is only a day's ride from here." Now both men were silent, and Oin slowly rose to his feet.

"Once more I beg pardon for the intrusion, but you have been most helpful. I am obligated to you." Hojo lowered his head as Oin bowed and quickly made his exit. Several minutes after his departure, Hojo still had not moved. His face wore a despondent expression as Kaoru walked into the room holding a bottle of rice wine. He handed it to his father and Hojo looked up smiling.

"Who was that man, father?" Kaoru asked.

"Another fool, running to meet his death," came the answer.

Outside, Oin walked against the wind, heading in the direction of the Shogun's castle. A light rain began to fall, sending an even greater chill into the air; Oin could now see his breath and, as he walked, he could hear a deep voice singing a melancholy chant as he passed the last houses of the village; and the scent of incense wafted into his nostrils as the people of the village sat down to pray at their shrines.

Xavier Takei stopped to rest against a fir tree. He rubbed his sore feet and cursed in a piously safe manner as the fallen needles of the tree poked through his robes and into his skin. He had been walking for hours, having snuck away from the palace, and his whole body seemed on the verge of collapse. He rubbed his feet, massaging and lamenting them until his hands became sore. Before he left the palace in a fit of desperation, he imagined the purity of his cause would keep hunger, exhaustion, and the fear of personal danger at bay; but apparently this was not the case, for he felt all three of these, and he suddenly began to wonder if he should not simply have stayed in the palace.

"I knew you would try something stupid like this," came the voice of Jacobin Endo, quiet and secretive in the dark, and Xavier nearly jumped out of his skin as he hid his body behind the fir tree.

"What are you doing here?" he asked in a high-pitched voice. Endo walked over to his spiritual father and stood before him. Takei looked up at him, and in his remembrances of Endo as a youth, crying at his feet and begging him to relieve him of his sins, he began to fear less and, almost instantly, he regained the firm countenance of the priest. Then, with a virility nearly forgotten due to old age, Takei rose to his feet and slapped Endo hard across the face. Endo recoiled like a spurned child and held his hand to his face which already began to redden. "Evil has found its way into your heart," said Takei. "And be careful lest it bleed into your soul as well!"

"Father," began Endo in earnest, "I do only what is right. There is cruelty, yes, but righteous are my motivations."

"Be silent!" said Takei, holding up his hand. "I fear you have yet to realize what countless innocent lives will be lost, and what a massacre you have let loose into being, the Lord save us."

"S-sacrifices must be made," said Endo, stammering over his words, and Takei turned away from him. Endo felt a great guilt in his heart, and he could imagine an all too real darkness beginning to envelop his soul, but then Takei began to walk, and it came to Endo that his deed would be all the darker if Takei were to do as he planned, and warn the boy and his father of the danger awaiting them. Not only would this enrage Shogun Shitaké, most likely causing him to change his policies on the Christians; it would also shine a bright light on the crime Endo himself had proposed. He would be known until his dying day for this. It would be better to let his part in the affair fade away, be hidden behind the horrors of the crime. And so Endo, overcome with both fear and determination, began to chase after Xavier Takei; and upon catching up with him, tackled the old priest to the ground. But this was a reflexive action not meant as an open act of hostility against the man who had brought him into the folds of the church with open arms and without judgment, and so Endo quickly jumped back to his feet, away from the old man, and stared down at him with wild but penitent eyes. Takei, however, continued to sprawl around on the ground, flailing his arms and legs wildly as if absolutely certain Endo was still attacking him. The dirt flew into the air, and the dead needles of the trees crunched loudly; and Takei seemed like a dog digging for a lost bone, foaming at the mouth and panting.

"Please forgive me!" yelled Endo, and Takei suddenly turned over to see him, not only standing, but at a safe distance some feet away and, grabbing the crucifix around his neck and pulling it from behind his robes, he held it out in Endo's direction.

"Back!" he moaned. "Get back or the devil take you!" At this, a hurt expression stretched across Endo's face, and he touched his hands to his chest as if he couldn't believe what Takei had just said to him.

"I cannot allow you to jeopardize the future of our community," Endo said with conviction. But Takei now began to crawl away, without the strength even to stand, and his breath grew even heavier. Endo watched the old man crawling away, and his heart was filled with pain for what he knew he must do. Slowly, hesitantly, as though his heart was just not in it, Endo walked until he came over to Xavier Takei; and then, sitting down on the old man's back, he began choking the life out of him, considering it a sad, though necessary, duty. As Takei's neck snapped, Endo was reminded of the sound of the old man's walking stick, tap-tapping on the ground in front of him as they walked the floors of the church together.

14

Lady Keiko had discovered a secret. It seemed to her that whenever her husband touched her while in an aroused state, she would stumble upon some new secret in the art of origami. Normally disgusted by her husband's touch, though she couldn't help an attraction to his power and strength. Lord Shitaké now found himself, more than ever, the pursuant of her charms. Though this did not usually end with his pleasure, as after the initial foreplay, Lady Keiko would run off to try and make the folds that had been revealed in her head. She was now sure, after several nights of disappointment for Lord Shitaké, that she would indeed take first prize at the contest.

So it was, with Lord Shitaké salivating and tossing the thought about in his mind of some sort of a leash or cuffs to keep his wife from running off this time, that Lady Keiko had revealed to her the "Hell Fold", which was a three-paper fold: orange, white, and red: that had the appearance of orange flames licking at a white-hot soul on a red plain. It was quite a difficult fold, and also quite new, being inspired by the recent teachings of the foreign Dutch traders; and Lady Keiko was almost certain that the hell fold would be virtually unknown in the province since Lord Shitaké, while giving fair treatment to the Christians, also made sure that their converts did not reach too great of a number by limiting most of their activities to the castle.

"Years ago," began Lord Shitaké as Lady Keiko once more rolled herself out from under the sheets in a slow, stealthily fashion, as if she hadn't caught onto the fact that Shitaké was perfectly aware of her ruse, having gone through it several times already in the last week, "I promised myself that I would not fall victim to your womanly ways. But unless you are with child, I demand you return to this bed!"

"I beg forgiveness my Lord," replied Lady Keiko. "But I have an urgent matter that must be attended to, I know in your heart you will understand." Lord Shitaké was caught off guard by this remark, and hesitated before continuing the argument, wondering if it would not be more honorable to let her attend to her business, and thus prove that his heart could indeed understand whatever it was. But he was not so easily ensnared.

"Whatever urgent matters you feel may need seeing to, I am the Lord of this palace, and I demand the filial duties of my wife at least. I, who rule all this land, have time for such things. How is it you have no time?"

"Would you have me forsake my duty to my girls?" asked Lady Keiko, forcing tears into her eyes, but feeling all the same a slight fear.

"What is it your girls need that is more important than the Shogun?" asked Lord Shitaké, enraged at this insult. "You push my limits. If you insist on leaving this bed for something so unimportant as to see if your girls can properly apply their cosmetics, then I will have them all banished from the castle grounds!" he screamed, jumping out from beneath the covers, his naked flesh convulsing. "I will have them drawn and quartered! I will have the flesh boiled from their bones! I will make war on all consorts, if you refuse me once more!" But Lady Keiko really had no care for her girls, all she cared about now was the origami, the contest; and though she felt a great affection for Chikako, she would not let the threat of her death stand in the way of her prize. Besides, she was quite sure Chikako would be safe from any wrath Lord Shitaké might unleash.

"I am sorry, I must go," she said quickly, and left the room just the same. Lord Shitaké stared once more in disbelief. Had a portrait been painted of him at that moment, his would have been a sad legacy.

"Keiko!" he yelled after her, as he did all the other nights, but she would not return, and he knew this. In his anger and frustration, Lord Shitaké yelled once more, kicked at the mattress, then grabbed up the sheets and threw them about the room. Breathing heavily, he tried to calm himself; but his anger was too great, and he lifted up the mattress and tossed it through the paper-screened walls. At this disturbance, several of the palace guard ran into the room, and froze at the sight of their master, naked and perspiring, his teeth bared like some wild animal.

"My Lord?" said one of the guards, his sword drawn, and Shitaké raised his hands in the air.

"I have not summoned you," he said. The guards looked around and then at each other; sheathed their swords; bowed and exited the room. Lord Shitaké could hear muffled laughter as they returned to their stations. He thought of having them executed, but the sight of several loose sheets of origami paper lying on the floor took his attention. He did not wonder how the papers had got there, and had even less of a suspicion of his wife; he simply stared down at them. Then, with a certain hesitancy, he knelt and began to fold one of the papers into the shape of a dog.

15

Kimitaké Oin always paid attention whenever riders approached, but he was very good at leaving the impression that he hadn't. So, it was the soldiers of Lord Shitaké who had been sent out on the hunt for the illegitimate child rode past him without a thought. Oin waited several seconds once they had passed before turning to see where they were heading. Right toward Saikako he determined, and then continued on his way. Still, it was a strange sight to see armored horsemen riding about, especially since there had not been any strife for the past several years; and Oin's thoughts turned to war, and he felt a great desire to follow the horsemen just on the off chance that there might be some glory he could take part in. But he could not put off his search for Toyama

Shōki; and the castle could be seen plainly in the distance; and so realizing how close he might be to the man, he suppressed the urge to follow the horsemen.

Hours later though, as he reached the top of the last hill, marking a downward journey the rest of the way to the castle, he caught sight of smoke in the distance coming from the area in which Saikako lay and, remembering the fear that seemed to hold that village, Oin quickly turned back, and ran there as hard and fast as he could.

He was horrified at what he found. The entire village had been put to flame and the people sat weeping around the ashes of their homes; but what shocked him most were the small boys lying dead on the ground: twelve of them, their bodies slashed to ribbons. The mothers of the children paced around the bodies hysterically, and the fathers balled their hands into fists, as if hating themselves for the knowledge they could do nothing to help them. Oin looked down at the bodies as the people of the village walked around in a daze, the heat from the still burning fires pressing against them, when he suddenly remembered the boy Kaoru and knelt down to see if any of the bodies was his. He looked closely, not sure if he would be able to recognize the boy at first sight. Some of the children's faces had been slashed, their skin shriveled at the edges of the cut, showing the pale flesh like that of a boiled fish; the Tendōns poking out like tiny blades of grass slowly rising after having been stepped on. But Oin did not find Kaoru; in fact, he did not even see the boy's father around. Surely, if the boy had been killed, his father would be there with the other fathers, balling his fists and shamed at his own powerlessness.

Slowly, Oin stood up, and began looking around for the boy and his father. A few of the o-fuda, having escaped from the flames that took the houses they were meant to protect, scattered in the wind.

"Maybe they escaped," thought Oin. And then he heard some of the people of the village begin to scream.

"They are coming back!" they shouted, and scattered just like the o-fuda. Oin looked up and saw the soldiers riding back, their swords drawn. Only Oin remained on the road as they brought their horses to a stop. One horseman, a soldier of some rank, with the Shogun's crest of a green dove on his helmet, rode up close to Oin, holding a scroll.

"We did not see you before," he said authoritatively, "when we made the villagers gather."

"I was not in the village at the time," Oin

responded. The soldier glanced down at Oin's sword.

"Do you belong in this village?"

"No."

"Then what is your purpose here?"

"I am on my way to the Shogun's castle," Oin answered.

"What business do you have with Lord Shitaké?" asked the soldier, and Oin noticed the other soldiers beginning to tighten around him, closing in on him, having dismounted their horses. He kept his hands from his sword, careful not to provoke them.

"I have no business with the Shogun. I am looking for a man. His name is Toyama Shōki. I was told he might be at the university."

"Then make your way there, and do not wander here," said the soldier. They were about to leave when Oin saw, not far off, Kaoru and his father, hiding behind the ruins of one of the houses. The soldier, seeing the change of expression on Oin's face, turned and saw them as well and, lifting his sword, he yelled to his men: "Get those two and bring them to me!"

At this, Hojo grabbed his boy and began to run, but the soldiers were quick to catch them. Oin watched, confused, as the soldiers ripped Kaoru from the hands of his father. Hojo tried in desperation to defend the boy against them, but they merely laughed and kicked him to the ground as Kaoru's cries pierced the air. Oin then looked once more at the bodies of the other children, then at the people of the village, who stood by doing nothing as Hojo begged for their aid.

Then, without thinking, and with great speed, Oin pulled his sword from its sheath and slashed the sword arm from the body of the commanding soldier. The others froze in their tracks, and the commanding soldier, shocked, stared down at the sight of his severed arm, blood spraying from the stump. Then, after some seconds of delay, he screamed in agony, and instinctively lashed out at Oin with the arm that held the scroll. Oin took a step back and, bringing his sword up, cut the commanding soldier from his third rib to his neck. The other soldiers still had not moved, too shocked at what they were seeing, as their commander fell dead before them. His body made a loud thump, and his blood splattered all those around him. Oin, who had not taken a breath throughout the whole encounter, now filled his lungs with air and turned toward the soldiers, his sword held high in readiness.

After a long, quiet wait, the soldiers finally began to move. There were twenty-five in all, and the most of them moved in cautiously, making a circle about Oin, but a few of them bounced around like intoxicated monkeys, their swords held high, undisciplined. Hojo ran and grabbed Kaoru, leading him away from the fight, and the people of the village gathered in a large group to witness the action.

Oin waited patiently for the attack as several of the soldiers' hurled insults at him, and feigned attack, hoping to draw him out of his defensive position. Oin had fought many men before this, but never quite so many as twenty-five at one time, and he soon began to look behind him, searching for a way to maneuver the men into a position that would enable him to take them on, if not one at a time, then at least no more than three; but the only surroundings were the burning huts of the village. Oin began to back up slowly, stepping between two burning houses; the embers hissed, and the flames served as two walls on either side. These licked at him, but his distance was far enough for it not to be too painful, and it served its purpose as a divider between the soldiers. Unless they were willing to jump through the flames themselves, they would have to come at him single file; though they could attack from both front and rear, his left and right were protected.

At last, the soldiers lost patience and attacked. Oin quickly defended, and took the first three soldiers easily enough, they being less cautious and so easily dealt with. But the smarter soldiers began working their way around the flames to attack from behind. Oin fought with intensity, and his defensive style was masterful. He tried to remain calm, but he could feel panic welling up in his heart. A single sword stroke caught him from behind, tearing through his kimono but causing little damage; yet blood dripped from the wound, and though he managed to take down four more of the soldiers, it looked as if the battle would soon be over. But then what he had feared would happen happened, though its effect was quite different than that he had feared. Three crazed soldiers, eager to partake in the fight, jumped right through the wall of flames rather than wait their turn and, luckily for Oin, these soldiers caused as much surprise to their fellows, that Oin was able to take the advantage. Quickly, as the soldiers in the line covered themselves, thinking they were being attacked through the flames, Oin cut them down two by two; then, grabbing one of the crazed soldiers, he pushed him in front of him back through the fire and, then once out, he cut the soldiers legs with a short stroke and pushed him back into the flames. The soldier screamed loudly as his body caught fire and, jumping from the ashes, he ran to and fro, hoping to put out the flames; and as he did this, the remaining soldiers panicked, trying to dodge their companion so that he wouldn't cause them harm in his predicament; Oin cut these men down too as they paid more attention to the burning soldier.

Soon there were only three soldiers left to do battle with Oin, and these three could hardly hold onto their swords as their hands shook with fright. Oin once more stood in a defensive position, and the soldiers hesitated. The sun was lowering behind him in the west, and the only light now remaining was that of the fire; and Oin, covered in blood, his clothes stained with mangled flesh and muscle, the fire shining in his eyes and on his sword, looked like one of the demons the soldiers' mothers had told them about in their youths, and death was no longer a far distant thing for them.

In unison the three soldiers raised their swords, and then, letting out a fierce cry, they attacked. Oin waited patiently as they ran at him and, once they reached him, quickly swung his sword, catching the three men before they could even strike out, and the legs of the men kept running for several yards after their torsos had fallen, spasmodically, to the ground.

16

Tiki Kōji saw the smoke coming from Saikako, but he was too busy contemplating the Golden Lotus to pay any attention. The announcement of the origami contest had spread far and wide, and Kōji had passed several groups already on their way to the castle. Some of the men he knew, and there were others whom he hoped to see upon arrival. Wataka Heiki, for instance, was an excellent paper folder, and came closer than most to being a fair rival to Kōji himself. But there were others that could be considered, if not rivals, then at least an honest challenge. But Wataka was the only man of whom the very thought could get Tiki Kōji's blood up and who, in fact, he oftentimes planned to kill. It nearly drove him insane that there could be somebody else out there who had a chance, no matter how small, of finding the secret of the Golden Lotus before he could. He would do just about anything to keep that from happening, even if it meant a few extra years of torment for Wei-Lei Ping.

The guards standing watch at the castle gates did not hinder Kōji's entrance through walls that were once meant to be defensive, but were now little more than decoration. Kōji looked around after stepping through the gates and thought bitterly of the times before, when the Lord Shitaké had not been so averse to showing his muscle, and Tiki Kōji was his top retainer. But Shogun Shitaké seemed much more interested in merely keeping the peace of late, maintaining the status quo. Kōji looked up where, sitting atop a hill, lay the Shogun's castle; and he remembered the days of glory that had once been his: taking an arrow in the right shoulder, saving the life of the Shogun himself. From that day on, he had been Shitaké's favorite and most trusted. But now the castle and all that surrounded it seemed like nothing more than an aged body without vitality; a once healthy frame that has ceased to exercise its muscle, turning to so much loose flesh.

But, although Kōji entered into the castle grounds with no trouble, it took very little time for his presence to be known. For suddenly, Kōji found himself confronted by several guards demanding he turn over his sword. Kōji stared the guards up and down, then looked up at the palace. Lady Keiko sat at one of the windows, staring down at him, a hateful look on her face. Kōji, smiling, bowed in her direction; after she left the window, he politely handed over his sword, knowing by this that the Shogun desired an audience with him. The guards took the sword and led him toward the palace. The guard holding the sword, while not outwardly afraid, could not help but wonder how much blood the blade in his hands had spilled.

"Tiki Kōji," said Lord Shitaké, sitting powerfully on his cushion at the far end of the room. Kōji remained standing, defiantly but for a faint glimmer in his eyes stemming from his love for the man. "What is it that brings you to these lands? Were you not exiled?"

"I was, my Lord. But I found news of the origami contest you are having, and you know I could not resist such a thing," said Kōji in response when, suddenly, Lady Keiko entered the room.

"I will not have this murderer in my home," she yelled, and Lord Shitaké laughed at his wife's nervousness.

"She was never too fond of you Kōji," he said, enjoying the frightened look on his wife's face, feeling that, somehow, it made up for her lack of physical affection the last few weeks. He would gladly see her brought to tears, scared out of her wits and begging for his protection. It would make up for his sexless life somewhat.

"The Lady has always been a self-willed person my Lord," said Kōji, laughing along with the Shogun and feeling very much as if there had never been a time of separation. Shitaké looked at his wife as she stood at the entrance, breathing so heavily he wondered she could keep her balance.

"What is it that disturbs you so?" he asked her, unaware of the true reasons for her worry.

"I only thought," she began, "that when this man was exiled, it was understood he was never to return. I only wish to know why he has disobeyed my Lord. And has it not been wondered, that on the day we receive news of the deaths of twenty-five of your loyal soldiers, Tiki Kōji makes his return?" Lady Keiko did not care for the deaths of the twenty five men, nor of any other deaths that might come about at Kōji's hands. All she cared about was winning the origami contest, and Tiki Kōji was as unbeatable at origami as he was at swordplay. She had come too far to be defeated now. She had to get him out of the way, somehow.

"Twenty-five of your men have been killed?" Kōji asked, genuinely shocked. Lord Shitaké lowered his head and sighed.

"Yes. It happened just this morning in Saikako village, not too far from here."

"What happened?"

"We are not sure," answered Shitaké.

"There is rumor," began Lady Keiko, smelling an opportunity, "that it was the work of a single warrior." Kōji looked over at her, confused.

"A single man, bringing down twenty-five of the Shogun's men? Who is this man?"

"We do not know," said Shitaké, loudly, signaling for her to keep silent. "As was said, it is only rumor."

"It is my opinion," interrupted Lady Keiko, "that if master Kōji would like to participate in the contest, then he should prove himself worthy of the Lord, by fulfilling the mission that the twenty-five soldiers failed to accomplish; and in so doing, he might even kill the man who committed that dark act." Kōji was now even more confused, but also intrigued. Things seemed to be much simpler before.

"One moment," Lord Shitaké said, then clapped his hands loudly. Seconds later, Jacobin Endo entered the room, wearing the robes of Xavier Takei, his hands wrapped around his crucifix. Kōji stared at Endo, and at the crucifix in particular, with a mild disgust. "What would you counsel?"

Shitaké asked Endo. Endo bowed his head and closed his eyes.

"I believe the Lady is correct, my Lord. If master Kōji would like to gain re-entrance into the heart of the Shogun, then he must prove himself worthy. And so long as the child lives, the Lord's future will be in doubt." Kōji was now even more confused.

"What child is it that this man speaks of?" he asked.

Hojo Ryu could not take another step. His body gave out thirty miles outside of Saikako.

"Father!" yelled Kaoru, kneeling before him. Hojo's breathing was heavy, and his body was covered with sweat. Oin, who had been leading the two, turned back and stood before the man. Tears poured from Hojo's eyes, mixing with the sweat and, though no tears came from Kaoru's eyes, the air was filled with his cries as he tried desperately to pull his father back to his feet. Oin laid a hand onto the boy's shoulder, understanding by the look in Hojo's eyes that he would not be rising again.

"Leave him be," he said calmly. Kaoru looked up at Oin and, feeling the strength coming from the man, he instantly calmed down, and gently placed his head onto his father's chest. Hojo had fought hard since the death of his wife to keep his spirit intact, but now all his strength seemed to have left him. Sensing that with the arrival of Oin his son would be safe, he now felt at peace with death, and longed to be re-united with his beloved Noriko.

"Kaoru," he said weakly. "You must be strong. Do not think of me when you are tested. You have a strength in your blood that you will never know."

"Father," cried Kaoru, tears finally rolling down his cheeks.

"Do not cry, my son. Do not let my last sight of you be one of grief." Hearing this, Kaoru calmed himself, and forced a smile. Hojo then looked to Oin. "I beg you to look after him. The Shogun's men will come again, and I fear they will not stop until he is dead." Hojo began to shake all over, and a white foam dripped from his mouth. Oin bent down low.

"Why does the Shogun want him dead?" he asked. But Hojo could keep death at bay no longer and, before he could answer, he closed his eyes for the final time, and the desperate heaving of his chest soon stilled.

"Father!" Kaoru cried once more as he thumped his fist on his father's chest. Hojo's body continued to spasm for some moments after the last beating of his heart, and the boy took this to mean there might still be life left in him. "Stop shaking, papa," he wept, but the body did not stop shaking. Kimitaké Oin stared off into the distance to see the Shogun's castle, and he wondered how many more soldiers could be out looking for the boy.

"You will not be able to mourn for long," he said. "If the Shogun really does want your life, then we must cast aside all needless emotion. Come stand by me and turn your head away." Kaoru wiped the tears from his face then, walking over to stand next to Oin, he closed his eyes. Oin first checked to see the boy was not looking and, with a single movement, he unsheathed his sword and thrust it into Hojo's chest. Kaoru, hearing the sick sound of pierced flesh and bone, suddenly opened his eyes and saw what had been done. With a gasp, he bounded away from Oin and dropped back down at his father's body.

"The body will be found. It is better if they think your father has died of some violence. With luck, it will slow their search." He then returned his sword to its sheath and lowered his hand to the boy. "Come, it will be dark soon." Kaoru took his hand and the two continued to walk, distancing themselves from Saikako and the Palace of Shitaké.

Lady Keiko, while walking about the palace grounds, marveled at the effectiveness of her scheming. A large pavilion was being constructed directly before the palace, and hundreds of small kiosks were being set up, with each arriving contestant serving their particular wares, specialty foods, children's toys; anything to cover the costs of their trip; and all of the kiosks seemed to have some kind of wooden placard above them, the owners hoping to win the contest and advertise their origami skills, and their desire to teach these skills to others willing to learn.

Suddenly the ground shook, and Lady Keiko turned to see fifty men, mounted on horseback, rising out of the palace grounds, Tiki Kōji riding with them. Before going out of the gates Kōji, having caught sight of her, turned and gave a smug bow. Lady Keiko returned his bow with an icy stare. He was aware of her intentions, and she knew it; and Kōji, being so supremely confident in his abilities, thought it no difficult matter to kill a lone warrior and a child, and then return to win the origami contest. But the contest was to take place on the following day, and she knew it would take at least that much time to find them and, if they could not, it would certainly take more than a day and a half to kill every seven-year-old boy in the entire province. Lady Keiko laughed as Kōji rode off with the other men, but as he did so, he lifted his hand in salute to an elderly man wearing nothing but rags, who sat cross legged on the dirt and watched the contestants setting up their kiosks; as Kōji did this, he gave Lady Keiko one last look, and the glimmer in his eyes spoke of a hidden advantage; then Lady Keiko could laugh no longer.

"Who is that man Tiki just saluted? Surely, he would not salute some ordinary beggar," she thought. She then made her way toward the elderly man and, standing before him, she rudely kicked at the man's bony knees.

"Who are you? Tell me your name quickly, for you may not be welcome here." The elderly man looked up, squinting his eyes to block the last rays of the setting sun, and said with a raspy, but confident, voice, "My name is Wataka Heike." And then a paper dragon, tossed by a child, landed at her feet.

Kimitaké Oin carried the boy Kaoru on his back. The boy slept soundly, exhausted, and his head bobbed gently in rhythm with Oin's steps. Oin had never before run from a battle and, in fact, a certain small disliking for the child had grown in his breast because of this. But Oin could not commit a dishonorable act. That, and, deep in his heart, as he felt the breath of the boy on the back of his neck, he knew what he was doing was right; and he discovered, then, that honor is not something to be gained from the battlefield only, and is not limited to the cause of death, but the cause of life as well.

The sun had long since gone down, and a bright halo of mist surrounded the moon. Oin knew it would be best to continue moving under cover of darkness, but fatigue had begun to set in; and so, kneeling gently, he placed Kaoru onto a soft bed of grass and lay himself against the trunk of a tree. He sat cross legged and closed his eyes, and quietly sang a sorrowful song. A large pool of collected rainwater sat off to his right, and the crickets made tiny splashes in the water as they jumped from the leaves floating upon the surface. Oin looked over at the boy, sleeping peacefully, and wondered at the mystery now facing him. Why did the Shogun want this boy dead? And to what lengths would he go to accomplish this goal? The dead children of Saikako added even more to the mystery. If the Shogun were so unsure of the boy's exact identity, so much so that he would have his soldiers massacre the children of an entire village, then what real threat could there be? Or had the Shogun become so corrupted by the long times of peace that he would actually create an enemy?

"How many children will die before he finds you?" Oin asked the sleeping boy under his breath. "Would it not be better for me to kill you myself?" He pulled out his short sword and let the moon's light reflect off it onto the boy's face, but then he became suddenly overcome with sleep and, still holding the blade, he closed his eyes and slept.

And while he slept, Tiki Kōji and his troupe were busy at work rounding up the villagers of Okakura. There were seventy-five children in all, but only thirty six between the ages of seven and nine. Tiki Kōji demanded the woman Hojo Noriko to step forward with her son, unaware that Noriko had thrown herself from the lighthouse, and that her son was now in the care of Kimitaké Oin; and when, after two minutes, Hojo Noriko did not step forward, he effortlessly cut down all thirty-six children, some of which were young girls, but Kōji cared very little for this. And when the mothers and fathers of the children began voicing their opposition to this cruel treatment, soldiers under Kōji's command began a slaughter ten times as violent and cruel as the massacre at Saikako. And the fires lit that night burned so bright it made the night as day.

When Kimitaké Oin awoke, in the haze of morning, he was taken aback by the slight scent of burning leaves in the air; and something else, oddly familiar, that he could not quite place. He then looked down and gasped as he saw the short blade in his hand, having forgotten his thoughts from before sleeping and, looking over, he noticed that Kaoru was no longer lying nearby.

"Kaoru!" he yelled, jumping to his feet.

"Over here," came an answer, and Oin then saw Kaoru leaning over the pond. Walking over to the boy, he knelt down next to him, and looked into the water. Tadpoles swam about the water in abundance, and several small lizards sat at the water's edge, hoping to catch a few of them for a small meal. Oin sniffed the air and wondered what the smell could be that seemed so familiar.

"You smell it too?" asked Kaoru. Oin looked down at him and nodded. Kaoru pointed off in the distance.

"It's coming from over there. I saw smoke this morning, but it isn't too bad now." Oin looked to where the boy pointed and could see thin wisps of gray smoke in the air.

"It has happened again," said Oin, wondering how high the death toll had risen while he slept.

"There are horsemen too," said Kaoru, tossing several blades of grass into the pond and watching the tadpoles scatter. "Heading this way."

20

Lady Keiko awoke with a great joy in her heart: the day of the contest had finally come. She looked to the east and saw the rising sun; the sky seemed to be separated into halves, and the red of the sun slowly overcame the blue of night. Lady Keiko poked her head from her window and saw, in every direction, the banners of the Shogun flying from every lookout post of the castle walls and, mingling with those were the tiny banners welcoming the contestants, many of whom had come from distant provinces.

The pavilion had been completed and several of the Shogun's retainers ran back and forth, ceremoniously setting up = the necessities of the competition. One hundred and thirty-two crimson pillows were laid out in a crescent shape; one for each of the contestants, who had entered their names the night before; and before each of the pillows was set a stack of papers of all colors. The papers were being equally administered; twelve of each color: red, orange, black, purple, green and white. And as the terms of the contest had already been agreed upon by three judges who had, as well, been chosen the night before, the number of shapes to be folded had already been decided. No contestant got a single sheet more than would be needed for the folds. If the contestant were to make a mistake, then that contestant would not be allowed to continue. The shapes were to be judged by likeness to the object and, also, the number of folds made to create the shape, and there were no time limits on the fold. All contestants were to wait until every other contestant had completed his folds, and then, afterward, the judges would make their inspections and determine who should continue, and who should drop out.

Lady Keiko had expected rules, but the predetermination of the shapes disturbed her. She had hoped to try out her Hell Fold in front of a crowd, but it being a new fold and quite regional, it was not likely the judges had chosen it. It was a small matter, though; for, as has been said, Lady Keiko had the utmost confidence in herself. Still, she couldn't help a nagging curiosity as to who

Wataka Heike was, and just why Tiki Kōji looked at her the way he did after seeing him; but she had little time for these questions as, with the breaking of the sun, the gongs were struck, announcing the preparation for the start of the contest.

21

Kimitaké Oin, with Kaoru, ran with all his might through the woods until, coming upon a clearing, he looked back and saw that not all the horsemen followed through the forest, only two outriders serving as guides. The outriders had spotted them earlier in the day, but Oin had lost them in the forest. Hiding behind a tree, he covered Kaoru's mouth, fearing the mist of his breath would give them away. Kaoru wheezed as he struggled to breathe through his nose but, his heart pounding from all the running, he tried to push Oin's hand away to breathe easier. Oin would not move his hand though, and Kaoru, panicking, began to cry.

"Quiet!" Oin said harshly, and just then, one of the outriders stopped his horse and tilted his head in their direction. Oin, very smoothly, drew his sword. Kaoru, seeing the sword, suddenly calmed himself, and the two of them peeked out from behind the tree to see how far the outriders were.

The pine needles crunched under the horses' hooves as the riders moved ever closer toward them, and Oin and Kaoru both held their breath. Kaoru shut his eyes tightly, but a strange curiosity for the event caused him to re-open them, and when he did this, he looked to his left and saw the muzzle of one of the horses move into his field of vision. Just as the horse moved forward, revealing the rider, Oin lunged, stabbing his blade into the man's kidney. The rider screamed in agony as he fell from his horse, and his armor, clanking against the trees, frightened his horse, sending it racing through the forest for its own safety.

The other outrider then came galloping toward them. Oin stood his ground and, when the rider came close enough, he took out his small blade and threw it. The blade flew straight and stuck in the rider's neck. The rider fell forward on his horse, and the horse slowed to a trot. Oin held onto his sword tightly with both hands as the horse rode past them with the rider hunched over on it, the blood from his neck pouring out, soaking the horse's mane.

It only took a few minutes for that horse to find

its way back to the others, and Kōji couldn't help but smile when he saw the pale-faced rider bent over the saddle. The rider's blood had turned the mare red, and Kōji felt satisfied at the prospects of immediate bloodshed just ahead. He ordered the soldiers, who had all been resting, to mount their horses, then led the way into the forest.

Kaoru took Oin's hand and walked with him into the clearing. Once out of the woods, the wind came at them forcefully, and Oin wrapped a cloth around his head to keep his hair out of his eyes. Up ahead was a lone hill, and atop that hill was a withered tree with many outreaching branches devoid of all foliage. There were the remains of some sort of masonry around the hill. A three-foot-high circle of brick surrounded the hill, and an overgrown path led to it. Oin followed this path.

"We will get to higher ground," he said to Kaoru. "We can use that wall to hide ourselves, and from there we should have a good view of the riders." Kaoru grasped his hand tightly.

"We cannot go there," he said, his voice shaking with fear and fatigue.

"Why not?" asked Oin.

"My father told me about that place. It is evil," he said, but Oin continued to lead them toward it. "He told me that, long ago, there was a demon living under that tree, and the Emperor used to send his bravest warriors out to destroy her because she did so much damage to the crops; but she killed them all easily. Until one day, a strong samurai from Kyoto came, and cut her deep in the belly, and after she killed him, she felt a great love for him because he was the only warrior who had ever cut her, and she put a spell on his soul, commanding it to return to her. But in order to cast the spell, she had to chop his body up and tie one piece onto every limb of the tree. And while she did this, she vowed never again to harm another human life."

"If she vowed never to harm another human life, then why do you fear this place so?" asked Oin, humoring the boy for his superstitions.

"Because the spell was a trick. It was taught to her long ago by the Demon Queller. He told her that one day she would fall in love with a mortal man, and that the spell would make him immortal, but really, it was a binding spell. And once the demon cut up the body of the mortal she loved and tied its pieces to the tree, she was to be trapped under the tree until the end of time. But her anger was so great at having been tricked, her evil essence can still bring harm to those that wander too close to the tree. That is why the tree has no leaves. Because nothing can grow on it." Kaoru shook as they reached the brick wall, and Oin lifted him up onto it.

"It is not a quelled demon you should be worrying about. It is the soldiers who are looking to kill you. Now get down behind the wall." Kaoru looked at the tree, then into the distance at the forest they had just come from; trying to decide which he feared most, the soldiers or the demon; but looking at Oin and feeling his confidence, he bent down behind the wall. Oin lay down on the wall and peered into the forest. No more riders had shown themselves, but he was sure they would come looking for their friends. It was inevitable that they would be caught, but at least with the higher ground, Oin and Kaoru would have a small chance of prolonging their escape. Oin watched and waited for some while until satisfied that the soldiers had ridden around the forest and were probably on their way to another village but, right as he let out a sigh of relief, he caught sight of the tree moving. Squinting his eyes, he lifted his head up slightly and, feeling no breeze, he ducked down again quickly.

Suddenly, the soldiers came into view at the edge of the clearing, pouring out of the forest like some vengeful phantom of nature. As the soldiers entered the clearing, they all lined up, and Oin counted them. Forty-nine in all, too many to even think about fighting. He looked over at Kaoru, who stared up at the tree with utter fear in his eyes. Oin looked up at the tree, himself, and was caught by the sight of the rotted rope dangling from every branch. He quickly looked away from the tree and back to the horsemen.

The horsemen stared in the direction of the hill but seemed to take little notice of it. Oin stared with wide eyes, praying to the gods that the soldiers would ride on in another direction. He held his breath in anticipation as the soldiers looked from left to right, until the one leading them, Kōji, pointed in a westerly direction. The soldiers slowly began to ride west, and Oin watched the seemingly endless line as they did so. He breathed another sigh, and looked back to Kaoru.

"They are going," he said, and Kaoru smiled with relief. But then, Oin saw something he was not expecting. At the end of the line of horsemen was a dark cloaked rider. Suddenly, Oin grasped the handle of his sword and, without a thought, jumped up onto the brick wall and, standing straight and drawing his sword, he shouted out, "Toyama Shōki! I am here!"

22

The contestants began taking their places, kneeling on the cushions; and all stared vacantly ahead at the piles of paper before them. The contestants were of all ages, from children to old men; some were women; including, of course, Lady Keiko, who took her place with a look of indignant pride. The people of the surrounding villages sat in a large grouping before the pavilion, and the Shogun's retainers sat behind them. Drinks were passed from one person to the next, and a small troupe of Korean acrobats performed their art, entertaining the crowd until the start of the contest. Several Dutch traders had also been invited to witness the spectacle, as well as several of their priests. The small Christian community of Shitaké's province sat surrounding the missionaries; all but Jacobin Endo, who was one of the judges chosen for the competition. He sat between the other two judges who were men of some consequence to the province.

After a short while, all one hundred and thirty-two contestants sat before their papers. Lady Keiko sat at the far right of the group, with Wataki Heike sitting at the opposite end, on the far left. Jacobin Endo stood up and faced the crowd and, holding up his hand, he signaled them for quiet. Once the crowd had been silenced, the first judge looked up and down the line at the contestants and, picking up a small card, he read aloud, "First fold: Frog!"

The contestants leafed through their papers, most choosing the green paper, but some, feeling risky, chose the orange; but before they could begin folding, a bell was rung, and the entire audience, as well as the judges and contestants, looked toward the palace, and saw Shogun Shitaké walking toward them. Two samurai walked by his side, and an old Shinto priest walked before him ringing the bell. They followed the Shogun to the pavilion where, to the amazement of the crowd, Lord Shitaké stepped up onto the platform and stood in the middle of the line of contestants. Those to his immediate left and right stared up at him in amazement.

The Shinto Priest ceased ringing the bell and, walking over to Jacobin Endo, he whispered something into his ear. Endo's eyes widened, and as the priest sat down behind him, he stood up and announced to the crowd, "A great treat, ladies and gentlemen: the mighty Lord Shitaké will bless us by taking part in this contest!"

The crowd let out a sound of amazement and Shogun Shitaké held out his hands, smiling. As he smiled, he looked over to the far end of the line and gave a piercing grin to his wife. Lady Keiko's eyes began to tear over and, with puffed out lips, she snorted at the mockery.

Tiki Kōji looked toward the hill and, seeing Oin standing there defiantly with his sword drawn, his lips parted in an evil smile. Then, pulling the sword from its sheath, he ordered the soldiers to attack.

Kaoru, not believing what had just happened, grabbed at Oin, trying to pull him down from the wall; but Oin stood his ground, waiting as the horsemen ran at him. The bells of the horses jingled and blended with the battle cries of the attacking horsemen, but Oin stood his ground, feeling the earth tremble below him. He did not fail to notice that Toyama Shōki did not charge along with the rest of the men; he simply watched and smiled, as if completely satisfied at the event taking place before him. As if it were all of his making. Kōji led the charge halfway to the hill, but soon fell back, allowing the others to move ahead, so that he might test this new opponent's mettle.

As the first wave of the soldiers reached the hill, they, in their frenzied states, misjudged the height of the brick wall, and so did not expect their horses to suddenly jump as they did. Oin froze with his sword in the air, and as the first riders' horses jumped past him, he quickly swung out at the falling men, killing three of them in mid-air. As their bodies fell, their blood hung in the air, creating a loose thread from their wounds to the tip of Oin's sword; and as the other soldiers approached, not falling into the same trap as their unfortunate companions, their horses trampled the bodies as they were reigned in. Oin, once again, took up his defensive position as the soldiers began riding in circles around the hill, taunting him, believing him an easy kill. Kaoru, thinking this to be the end and searching for any way out he could, began to climb the withered tree. The higher he climbed, the larger the host of soldiers seemed. A great cloud of dust mixed with grass flew into the air as the soldiers continued to circle. Kaoru could not believe the noise of it all, and was amazed at how Oin could just stand there, unflinching. He climbed all the way to the top and braced himself so as not to fall. Wrapping his arms around a short branch, he gasped as he saw how close his hands were to a knot of rotted rope, and he tried not to imagine what part of the warrior's body that rope had bound. Suddenly, the tree began to creak under him and, as he froze for fear of the branch breaking, an arrow flew by, narrowly missing his head, cutting the air and screaming in his ear. As he instinctively jumped back, the tree began to groan, there came a loud crack, and Kaoru suddenly felt himself falling.

"Frog," said the judge once again, as soon as Lord Shitaké had made himself comfortable; but no sooner was the fold announced, that one hundred and thirty of the competitors stood up and politely bowed out of the contest, not wishing to play against the Shogun. The only remaining contestants were Lady Keiko, Wataki Heike and the Shogun himself. Lady Keiko watched in disbelief as the contestants left the platform with emphasized speed, and took their places amongst the spectators.

"My one chance to prove myself and he has ruined it," thought Lady Keiko, shooting a scornful look at Shitaké. Lord Shitaké stared back at her, showing no emotion on his face, and calmly choosing a green paper with which to fold a frog. Lady Keiko locked eyes with him for some seconds, and she had to fight the urge to walk over and slap his face.

"Done," said Wataki Heike, holding out a

masterful fold of a frog, and Lady Keiko quickly looked in his direction, hatred in her eyes. Then, Lord Shitaké and Lady Keiko once more locked eyes, and began passionately folding frogs of their own.

"Done!" they both yelled out at the same time, showing off their folds. The Shogun's fold was rather basic, but nonetheless, had the appearance of the requested amphibian. Lady Keiko's, however, was a very neat fold, and Wataki Heike nodded his approval. The judges peered closely at the origami and then, deliberating amongst themselves for a short moment, announced the winner of the first round.

"We hold witness," said Endo, standing and addressing the crowd, "that the Lord Shitaké has folded the perfect frog!" The crowd broke out in applause.

Oin blocked and dodged the occasional sword thrusts of the soldiers and, although they were only halfhearted, taunting attempts, he felt his heart pounding: and a slight quiver shook his body as he felt the closeness of the blades. The main body of the soldiers continued to circle the hill, and Oin remained motionless atop the wall; but the circling soldiers were merely diverting Oin's attention from the single rider who had managed to dismount and work his way behind him. The single soldier raised his sword high and prepared to strike when the eighty-seven-pound body of Kaoru suddenly fell screaming down upon him, followed by the broken limb of the tree. Kaoru rolled off the soldier, unhurt, and Oin suddenly turned and jabbed his sword into the man's chest. The soldier screamed, blood shooting from his mouth and staining his teeth, and Kaoru ran to hide behind the trunk of the tree. Oin pulled his sword free and ran back to the wall where he quickly dropped to one knee and, with a long, single sword stroke, he took the heads off five circling riders who, having become so intent in the circling of the hill, had ceased to pay attention to their prey.

Their heads popped off and fell bouncing on the ground, but their horses continued to circle, and the headless bodies spewed blood from the stumps of the necks, spraying all those riding behind them. One soldier, angered by this sudden shower of red, quickened his pace, pulling alongside the bodies, and kicked them over, sending them rolling after their heads. He then jumped off his horse and ran screaming at Oin, who easily blocked the soldier's thrusts and attacked with his own blade, slashing the soldier first in the chest and secondly in the back as he then turned round with the force of the first blow. Tiki Kōji tilted his head back in laughter as he watched from a distance. Toyama Shōki, however, still had not left the cover of the forest.

"We hold witness, that the Lord Shitaké has folded the perfect monkey!" Endo yelled to the crowd. In fact, the Shogun's fold was a very bad one, and more closely resembled a dog. Lady Keiko huffed and stared, alternating her wide eyes from her monkey and Lord Shitaké's, unable to believe her luck.

Wataki Heike's monkey was a very fine one, and if Lady Keiko had been forced to choose a favorite over her own, she would have had to choose his as the perfect monkey. However, when she looked over at him, hoping to find an ally in her disgust over what was happening, she became even more upset at seeing the calm expression on his face; his appearance seemed even more prideful.

But even though the judges, and the crowd, were too intimidated to voice their opinions on the poorness of Lord Shitaké's folds, it was not lost on them; and toward the back of the audience could be heard certain murmurings dealing with the mindset of the Shogun, and some could be heard speaking of sexual frustration.

"The next fold," said Endo, picking up a card and reading, "will be the Hell Fold!" The words echoed in Lady Keiko's ears, and she gasped. Once more, she looked at Wataki Heike, and by the look on his face, she was sure that this was one fold he did not know.

Oin now found himself in the heart of a frenzied storm. His one advantage was the sheer number of his enemy for, to get to him, they had to first get by one another; but he was still only one man, and by the time he defeated one opponent, there was another to face. The battle seemed to be on some sort of a time joint in his mind. Even though it all went about quickly, so quickly he didn't have time to think, once an enemy was dispatched, the scene would be replayed in his head so that if he had had time to think at all, he would have been amazed at his own capabilities.

Oin fought with one soldier who, if he had not been a member of a force, would have been a great match for him. Desperately, he blocked the soldier's furious strokes; but in one of those instances of sheer reflex action, he managed to evade the sword stroke of the soldier that had ridden up behind him while engaged with the other and, ducking low, cut the forelegs out from under the horse. The horse gave out a heart wrenching scream as it crashed to the ground, the bells on its saddle jingling together, and the rider hurled forward onto the other soldier. It was a masterful stroke of luck that the two soldiers managed to impale one another on each other's swords.

Oin then took cover behind the wounded horse

as the remainder of the small army closed in. The horse no longer screamed out in pain, but its limbs writhed, and blood sprayed in thick torrents. Oin was exhausted, and the soldiers began to fear him. They approached closely, breathing hard, wild faces of battle giving way to the calm, steely glare of certain death, and Oin held his sword out with both hands, waiting, while the horse gave its death rattle below him.

Jacobin Endo and the two other judges sat in silence, and all three made a collective gulping sound in their throats.

"I am sorry my Lord," said Endo, his voice quivering, "but, we agree, that the Lady Keiko has best demonstrated the Hell Fold." After hearing this, Lord Shitaké crossed his eyes in anger, and looked at his wife. Lady Keiko smiled at him in return, and then looked to Wataki Heike. Wataki had not been able to make the fold, and his manner bespoke his slight loss of pride. Nonetheless, he did bow to Lady Keiko, and portray at least a begrudging respect for her abilities.

Lady Keiko could not help but smirk. Humility being totally unknown to her, she could not wait for the next fold to be announced, now believing Lord Shitaké's hold on the contest to be in doubt; and Heike had yet to win the favor of the judges on any of the folds.

"Ha!" she said a little too loudly, and each and every member of the audience looked at her. She then lowered her head in embarrassment, and, with her eyes shielded by her hair, she stole a glance back at her husband. He had made so many mistakes, he had begun working off of one of the piles left by a former contestant. "He should have been disqualified already," she said under her breath, and sneered.

"The next, and final fold will be," Endo said loudly, playing up the suspense felt throughout the crowd; and Lady Keiko was about to remark on how the contests had not gone through the designated number of folds; but before she could do this, Endo screamed dramatically, "the Golden Lotus!" She did not see the sun glinting off Wataki Heike's teeth as his mouth opened in a wide smile.

Oin dispatched twelve more of the soldiers with a minimum of difficulty, but it began to appear as if there would be no end to them. At this point Kōji joined the fray. Kaoru screamed out a warning, but not before Kōji's blade cut deep into Oin's back. Oin instinctively jumped forward and gave a backward slash, missing Kōji by some feet, nonetheless, forcing him to keep his distance.

Oin could feel his skin separate where it had been cut by the razor thin blade, and a heat flowed through his entire body. Through blurry eyes he watched Kōji approach him, and it was only by a stroke of luck that he was able to lift his sword in time to block Kōji's swing, which would have taken his head.

Kaoru, feeling a bravery far beyond his years, picked up several pieces of the broken tree limb and began hurling them at Kōji. Kōji, laughing, reached back, and struck Kaoru with the back of his hand, sending him reeling over the knotty roots of the tree. Oin could barely stand as the thirteen remaining soldiers moved in on him. He tried to stand but dropped to his knees. Blood flowed from his wound, reddening his kimono. Kaoru rolled over on the ground and took what he thought must have been a final look at Oin. Oin stared back at him, weakly.

"I have put your life in jeopardy," said Oin. "I am ashamed of myself." Kaoru shook his head, and tears began to flow from his eyes as the tragedy of the situation began to make itself clear to him. This man Oin had faced an army, yet he was going to die feeling like a failure.

At the edge of the clearing, Toyama Shōki looked on, and frowned.

Kōji slowly walked toward Oin and, quite without effort, lifted his sword for the final blow, when Oin, not giving into death, jumped to his feet and, moving in a wide circle, cut down the remaining thirteen soldiers. Kōji jumped back with a look he had never before shown: a look of fear. He froze as the bodies of the soldiers fell down in the same circular pattern they had stood, and then he stared wide-eyed at Oin as he pointed his sword directly at him.

"I am Kimitaké Oin," he began, "son of Kimitaké Osugi from the province of Encho, and I challenge you." At the edge of the clearing, Toyama Shōki smiled.

Lord Shitaké crumpled up his fourteenth piece of paper in his attempts to fold the Golden Lotus and, leaning his head in the direction of his wife, saw that it was not a fold known to her either. Lady Keiko could not understand what was happening. She had been studying and practicing the art of origami for some time now, yet she had never heard of the Golden Lotus fold. She began simply enough, by folding a traditional lotus blossom, but when she looked over at Wataki Heike, it was obvious she was not on the right track; for he seemed completely confident in his folds, and in fact, seemed to utterly enjoy the process. As much as she hated the thought, she knew she would have to mimic Heike's folds.

Carefully, she began to copy Heike's

movements, even going so far as to mimic the man's ceremonial manner; but Heike had caught on, and began making folds, and then undoing them three folds later. Of course, these were folds meant to be undone by him, and so he had not creased the paper. However, Lady Keiko had not expected this and, having creased the paper, she was forced to start over with a new sheet until, suddenly enraged, she jumped up from her cushion and, pulling a short dagger from her kimono, she plunged it into the old man's heart.

Lord Shitaké, as well as the audience, gasped in horror as Wataki Heike coughed, and crouched over his stack of papers.

"Keiko!" screamed Lord Shitaké, but Lady Keiko was not of her own mind any longer, having been driven insane by the thought of somebody defeating her so easily at something she had striven at for so long. Heike coughed again, and blood poured from his mouth.

"I was-so close," he whispered in Lady Keiko's ear before passing on. Lady Keiko stared out into the crowd with a look of complete insanity. The judges of the contest, who had all risen to their feet, merely stared stone faced at her. They looked at Lord Shitaké, and then back to her. Then, Jacobin Endo announced to the crowd, "We do hereby attest, that the mighty Lord Shitaké is the winner of this contest!"

"No!" screamed Lady Keiko, clutching her chest with one hand, and pulling her hair with the other. "No! You cannot do this! I do not accept this! I do not!" She continued to tear at her hair until, falling to the floor, she lay next to the gurgling body of Wataki Heike. His blood flowed, mixing with her hair, and she slowly lay her face down into it as her tears flowed. Shogun Shitaké, quite embarrassed, motioned to his retainers; two of them moved forward, lifted Lady Keiko up, and carried her to the palace. Her cries were drowned out by the Shinto priest's bell as he began to lead the crowd away from the pavilion. The contest had ended the only way it could have, and Lord Shitaké had one of his men send for the girl Chikako so that he might be comforted for the loss of his wife.

Oin and Kōji stood apart; both holding their blades in a defensive position. Kaoru held his breath, safely watching from behind the tree. In the distance, Shōki watched as well, his hand resting calmly against the hilt of his sword. Oin slowly began to move. He lowered his sword, tilting it toward the ground and, moving in a wide arc, crept closer to Kōji. Kōji tensed the grip on his sword and began to move in the same pattern, until both men circled one another, steely eyes watching, waiting. Then Oin stopped and dug the heel of his right foot into the ground. Kōji, nerves on edge, and always more of an offensive fighter, grabbed his sword with both hands and, holding it high, gave a shrill, primal scream and charged toward Oin. Kaoru shut his eyes tight with Kōji's scream echoing in his ears and tried not to imagine what would happen to him once Oin was dead.

Kōji ran at Oin with great speed, his scream getting louder as he approached. Oin stood still, patiently waiting, sword still pointed at the ground. Finally, Kōji got within striking distance. The muscles in his arms and shoulders tensed as he readied to bring his sword down on Oin's head; but then he suddenly felt an icy coldness run through his body and, looking down, he saw that Oin had already cut a huge gash into his stomach.

Kōji stood still before Oin; his sword still high in the air, having never brought it down; and he looked down at his wound. Oin's attack had been so quick he never saw it coming. He spit blood, and his intestines began to unravel, spilling out of his belly. Oin now had his sword pointed toward the sky, a single drop of blood lay on the point, and he waited patiently for Kōji to fall. Kōji let out a ghastly moan before falling to the ground. He lay at Oin's feet, writhing in agony; his hands still clutched around the handle of his sword.

Kaoru opened his eyes and, relieved, he ran to Oin and hugged his leg. Oin gently pushed him away for Kōji still lived. He looked down at Kōji, then toward the forest and saw Toyama Shōki riding toward them. Kōji's body continued to spasm on the ground, as if he believed he could end his pain by pushing it from his stomach to another part. He moaned as his body convulsed, and all he could think about now was the Golden Lotus. With a great strength of will, he reached into his kimono and pulled out a sheet of white paper that had become stained with his own blood. Oin bent down and watched curiously as he began to fold it. Kōji's fingers' shook as he tried to stay alive in order to complete the fold and, Oin, moved by this strength, bent down next to him and gently helped to fold the creases of the paper that Kōji could no longer accomplish.

Toyama Shōki arrived and, dismounting his horse, he stood next to the two men and watched. Even Kaoru had knelt next to Kōji, feeling a certain admiration for the man. Kōji locked eyes with Oin and he began to cough from the blood filling his throat, choking him. Suddenly, he grabbed Oin's hand, gripping it tight. Oin stared down at him and witnessed the last breath of Tiki Kōji. He then looked down at the paper; it was a strangely shaped box, but it was incomplete.

"The Golden Lotus," said Toyama Shōki, his voice clear and calm. Oin looked over his shoulder at him, no longer having a desire to fight the man.

"What is it?" he asked.

"It is the perfect fold," answered Shōki. "Yet, this one is not finished." Oin looked back at the paper box.

"How can it be finished?" he asked. Toyama Shōki bent down and, lifting one of the corners of the box, he folded it out, breaking the angular pattern of the square shape.

"The Golden Lotus," began Shōki. "It is the closest representation of the human soul. It is so simple, yet there are only a few who have mastered its secret." As he spoke, he grabbed Oin's hand and placed it onto the box, helping him to fold a piece back from the opposite side as that he had done. "It is a fold that can only be made at the moment of death." When Oin folded out his corner, a gust of wind blew over him, and it sounded as if the earth were sighing, a long life finally at peace.

Toyama Shōki then stood up and stared down at Oin. "Wei-Lei Ping is now at rest," he said. "This man was your rival Kimitaké Oin. Your demon has been vanquished. Now you may know peace as well." After saying this, he mounted his horse and began riding away at a slow pace. Oin stood and watched him leave.

"Who are you really?" he yelled after him; but he got no answer. Shōki rode back to the forest and disappeared. Kaoru looked up at the withered tree and shivered. The sight of the tree made him more uneasy than the pile of dead bodies before him.

"Can we leave this place?" he asked, as Oin, taking his hand, began leading him away.

"Come," he said calmly. "We must bury your father."

Kaoru would never know what all the violence had been about, why all those lives were lost; because Kimitaké Oin would never tell him; choosing instead to lead the boy to peace and enlightenment. And so, they walked away from the scene of the battle, quietly, sullenly, amidst the stink of blood and horse sweat. The wind blew across the field, laying low the grass and creaking through the branches of the haunted tree, jingling the ornaments hanging loosely from the armor of the fallen soldiers; examples of superstitious good luck charms that proved incapable of warding off the grim reality of a warriors violent death; until finally, the wind, playfully hovering above the scene, picked up the Golden Lotus, and carried the souls of Wei-Lei Ping and Tiki Kōji to the end of forever.

THE END

"Myomōtō Kōji reached the outerlands of Lord Shitakē..."

www.ingramcontent.com/pod-product-compliance
Lightning Source LLC
Chambersburg PA
CBHW072001170626
46813CB00005B/1958